SHOOT, RUN OR DIE!

Cody had once fought a cougar to a standstill — bare-handed. He's not a man to mess with. When Curtin and Willis rob him, leave his partner parboiled and burn down the cabin, there is nowhere for the killers to hide. Now a whole town want him for their sheriff — all but Deputy Blake Ross. He makes more trouble for Cody than he's ever seen, enough to plant him on Boot Hill with men he had hunted and killed.

Books by Jake Douglas
in the Linford Western Library:

LAREDO'S LAND
RIO GRINGO
RIO REPRISAL
QUICK ON THE TRIGGER
A CORNER OF BOOT HILL
POINT OF NO RETURN
SUNDOWN
SIERRA HIGH
JUDAS PASS
LOBO AND HAWK
RIDER OUT OF YESTERDAY
SOUND OF GUNFIRE
HALFWAY TO HELL
NORTH FROM AMARILLO
TOO MANY SUNDOWNS

JAKE DOUGLAS

◆

SHOOT, RUN OR DIE!

Complete and Unabridged

LINFORD
Leicester

First published in Great Britain in 2009 by
Robert Hale Limited, London

First Linford Edition
published 2010
by arrangement with
Robert Hale Limited, London

British Library CIP Data

Douglas, Jake.
   Shoot, run or die!- -(Linford western stories)
   1. Revenge- -Fiction. 2. Western stories.
   3. Large type books.
   I. Title II. Series
   823.9′2–dc22

   ISBN 978–1–44480–435–5

Published by
F. A. Thorpe (Publishing)
Anstey, Leicestershire

Set by Words & Graphics Ltd.
Anstey, Leicestershire
Printed and bound in Great Britain by
T. J. International Ltd., Padstow, Cornwall

This book is printed on acid-free paper

1

Man-Hunter

He walked in out of the night rain leading a horse with a dead man draped across the saddle.

Marsden was the first to notice him, just standing in the lee of a big rock with the rain drumming on his worn poncho and streaming from his hatbrim. He was holding a rifle in his right hand, barrel down to keep out the water.

The stranger nodded briefly when he saw he had been noticed, and Marsden said quietly to his two companions squatting by the small fire, 'Visitor.'

They swung around fast, Carter dropping his tin mug of coffee, hand slapping his gunbutt. Franklin, short and broad, just stared, running the tip of a pink tongue around thick lips.

1

'Kinda wet,' the stranger offered, not raising the rifle.

Carter let his hand remain on his gunbutt. 'Who's that?' he asked hoarsely, nodding towards the blurred shape of the horse and its burden.

'Dead man.'

'You shoot him?'

The visitor nodded. 'Outlaw — went by the name of Ed Curtin.' The voice was deep, slightly hoarse. 'Looking for his sidekick: calls himself Willis — Carter Willis.'

Marsden and Franklin both looked sharply at Carter and slowly moved away from him. They couldn't see the stranger's face, shadowed as it was by his dripping hat-brim, but they knew his eyes were boring into Carter.

Carter knew it too, and lunged to his feet, hesitating with six-gun half-clear of leather.

'Shoot, run, or die, mister!' the stranger invited.

'Reckon I'll shoot!' Carter said, voice breaking as he whipped up his Colt, lunging to one side.

'Then die.'

The stranger's rifle crashed with a bellowing noise whipping through the small camp, echoing from the big rock behind him. Carter was hurled back, twisting mid-turn, and sprawled face down in the mud beside the small fire.

Ears ringing, astonished at the speed the stranger levered in a fresh cartridge, the other two lifted their hands slowly.

'Ea-easy, mister!' grated Marsden. 'We're outriders for the Busted K spread. C-Carter just started with us couple weeks back.'

'That'd be about right. I've been trailing them both for a month. They split up a couple of weeks ago.'

'Lawman?'

Water fanned from the hat-brim as the man shook his head. 'I'll take Carter's horse: he can ride alongside his pard.' He didn't have to indicate the dead man.

'What happened to your horse?' asked Franklin.

'Curtin shot it; left me afoot in the desert.'

'If you ain't a lawman,' queried Franklin slowly, 'what are you?'

'Had a difficulty with these two — I aim to claim any bounty on 'em. Need the money. Now, how about pointing me in the direction of the nearest town? After you pour me a cup of coffee — OK?'

The cowboys stumbled against each other as they both reached for the smoke-black pot simmering at the edge of the coals.

The manhunter stepped into the fireglow, throwing one careful look at Carter's body, pushed back his poncho flaps, and took the mug of steaming coffee. He sipped, smacked his lips.

'Pretty good for range coffee. Town far?'

'Day and a half, two days' ride,' Marsden told him. 'We're a long ways from ranch headquarters here . . . Like I said, outriders, searchin' for strayed cows wearin' our brand.'

The visitor nodded, sipped again. They couldn't see much of his face in the dull glow, but the impression was one of hard, strong features under a three-day stubble.

'What's the town called?'

'Hopeful.'

They saw his mouth soften.

'Sounds promising.'

★ ★ ★

As a concession to Sheriff Nate Palmer and his new bride who was returning to Hopeful, the Concord stage had been newly painted. The new bodywork colour was a kind of dull red, which had resulted because there wasn't enough of either bright red or black. So the company had mixed the two.

The colour was acceptable and with the thin yellow lines running fore and aft, curling and dipping, the window frames edged in white and dark green, the overall effect was pleasing.

Not that the lawman and his bride,

Ellie, cared that much. Like the other three passengers, all they wanted to do was reach Hopeful with a minimum of bruises and mostly in one piece. It was hot and dusty, despite the canvas blinds, and the driver, Arrowhead Benson, had been celebrating the nuptials as if the bride and groom were family: he seemed to hit every rut.

The shotgun guard, Topeka, riding alongside him, clung to the newly painted iron rail at his side — not yet dry and staining his fingers — his shotgun in his other hand as the stage swayed and rocked and bounced over the winding trail coming down from the Bitterroots.

'Go back! You missed one pothole! Damn you!'

Benson, singing, winked at Topeka, his voice was so slurred only he knew what he was saying.

Until, suddenly, he hauled on the reins so violently, he was yanked out of his hard plank seat, half-standing, as the team mouthed the wrenching bits, whinnying and swerving with the abrupt tension he threw on the long leather lines.

'Ho-ly Jes-*us*!' The driver staggered, almost falling down on to the rumps of the rear horses, ending sprawled across the guard's lap.

'Goddammit, Arrerhead! What the hell — ?'

'Lookit, you blind idiot! *Hold-up*!'

The guard struggled free, pushing the driver away, lurched to his feet, bringing up his long-barrelled Greener. He spotted the three horsemen on the trail, sun glinting from their gun barrels. Topeka lifted the Greener, thumbing the right-hand hammer, but that was as far as he got.

Two shots from the riders and he fell limply over the side to lay in the dust by the front wheel on that side.

Arrowhead Benson, standing upright now, swaying, lifted both hands, holding the rein ends in his left one.

'Don't shoot!' Those words were clearly understood, too, and one of the

7

men walked his horse forward, a bulky man with long fair hair hanging raggedly from under his hat. He had a rugged face, covered in dust from hard riding.

'Throw down that strong box,' he ordered, lifting his smoking pistol.

While the driver struggled to get the iron-bound chest out from under the seat, the fair-haired man called, 'You folk in there, step on down. We is feelin' hos-*pit*-able — right, boys?'

'Right as rain, Arnie!' agreed one of the riders, the one with the peaked sombrero. 'Right as always.'

The man next to him, called Dack, hissed through his teeth, 'You damn fool! No names!'

The man in the peaked hat paled and swung towards the fair-haired man — too late. Arnie shot him dead, then turned back to the stage as the strongbox thudded to the ground. He triggered a shot, the bullet ripping a long sliver out of the roof edge of the coach.

'You in there! Let's take a look at

you! Pronto, now!'

The fat drummer from Arkansas, peddling some kind of marvellous snake oil, was first to puff his way out. He came with hands raised high, sweating and wheezing, roly-polying clear of the stage, making sure the road-agents saw he was not going to give any trouble. He had already wet his pants and dropped to his knees, clutching at his chest and toppled over as the guns swung towards him. Faint or heart attack, no one knew — nor seemed to care right at that moment. He lay there in the shadow of the stage, twitching, a little froth on his lips. Next out was the lean banker. He turned to help down his sobbing wife, with her new corsets hour-glassing her large waist painfully, and congesting her face with their torturing constriction.

Inside, remained only the newly-weds, Sheriff Nate Palmer and his blushing bride. He had already removed his brass star from his vest, tugged the jacket across so as to hide the holes pricked through the cloth.

He stepped out and, without even glancing at the road-agents, helped his bride down. A vagary of wind flapped the hem of Ellie's skirt and a well-turned ankle flashed. The robber called Dack whistled through his teeth. Big Arnie was staring at Palmer.

'I know you.'

'Never met,' the sheriff said flatly. He was a raw-boned man in his early forties, bore a few facial scars from past fights in the course of his duty. *But he knew Arnie Kelsey from seeing the man's face on several Wanted dodgers.* He felt a tightening of his stomach: this robber was well known for his amorous interest in women — young and old. *And Kelsey was no gentleman . . .*

Ellie, years Nate's junior, clung tightly to his left arm. He flexed his bicep, trapping her fingers, reached across and patted her hand, smiling comfortingly. 'It'll be all right, me darlin', just do exactly as they say and everythin'll be all right . . . ' He lifted his gaze to the fair-haired man and could have bitten out his tongue as he added carelessly, 'Ain't that so, Kelsey?'

'So! You do know me, you son of a bitch!'

Ellie gasped and Palmer knew by the sudden increased weight on his arm that her legs had almost given way. The man peered closely and swore bitterly, his choice of expletives bringing a loud, shocked howl from the banker's wife.

Arnie Kelsey ignored her, frowning at Palmer. 'Hell, yeah! You're the sheriff of Hopeful! Nate Palmer. Well, well, well. I almost don't care how much is in that strongbox now you're here — almost!' He chuckled. He winked at his companion. 'Got me a bonus here, Dack. Recollect I tol' you about that time down in Laredo when a fat-bellied cowman had my kid brother strung up for runnin'-ironin' one of his steers? Well, this sonuver was his foreman then! He tied the hangman's knot, hauled young Riley up an' let him hang-'n'-rattle!'

Ellie wailed and sagged against Palmer who struggled to hold her. Kelsey stepped in and swung his gun, the barrel knocking off Palmer's buff-coloured hat, breaking the skin at the hairline above his left eye. Ellie fainted dead away, sprawled in the dust as the sheriff fell to his knees, gasping, dazed.

The banker's wife swooned also and the man was hard put to support her weight and lower her gently to the ground. Then a whip cracked and stinging thongs wrapped themselves about Arnie's gun arm, yanking him around violently, his gun dropping from suddenly numbed fingers.

Dack's gun crashed in two fast shots and Arrowhead Benson toppled from the high driving seat, the whip butt falling from his lifeless hand. His body landed across the rumps of the rear team horses and, nervous already, they lunged away with snorts and whinnies. The stage lurched, bounced over the body of the shotgun guard — and the banker made his play, reaching under his coat for a short, over-and-under derringer.

Kelsey, wrenching the whip thongs from around his arm, thrust the dazed sheriff to the ground as he scooped up his Colt and shot the banker even as the man fired the little weapon. The banker fell over his sprawled wife's body and Dack, still mounted, cursed as the small ball clipped his right shoulder.

Straightening, Arnie Kelsey's brown eyes seemed to blaze with deep-set fire as he put his gaze on the lawman who had one hand down in the dust, supporting him. Ellie began to stir. Arnie Kelso grinned.

'Hey, Sheriff, don't pass out on me. Things are just startin' to get reee-al interestin'!'

Smirking, he leaned down and ripped the unconscious Ellie's bodice down to her waist.

Dack sucked in a sharp, audible breath. '*Man*! Lookit 'em!'

'See what I mean, Palmer?' Kelsey stooped over the lawman. 'I'll bet you stood by an' rolled a smoke while young Riley danced his jig at the end of your rope, huh?'

'I'd do without the smoke to see you dance the same kinda jig, Kelsey.'

Arnie smiled without mirth. 'Well, I never was much of a dancer. But I'll bet that new bride of yours can do some high kickin' . . . ' He paused and drove a boot into the side of the sheriff's neck. 'An' you're gonna live just long enough to watch. Ain't that somethin' to look forward to?'

2

Hopeful

It was just after noon on the second day after leaving the outriders' camp, when the man-hunter entered Hopeful.

The town didn't impress him much; it was smaller than he expected, yet, at the same time, there was something about it that made it a little different to the usual weathered frontier town. And that was it — it didn't have the scoured, faded look of the frontier towns he knew. The buildings still showed traces of fresh wood in places that hadn't been painted over; all the glass he could see, in shop fronts and windows of houses fronting Main, was intact, maybe one in a saloon had a crack wriggling across. The roof gutters were neither rusted nor sagging and the shingles hadn't yet taken on that dull, neutral look from

15

the scorching western sun.

This town was tolerably new, he allowed, and there was one more thing: there was no traffic.

No rolling wagons, or stages drifting in to the depot, riders heading for streetside hitch rails, though there were a few saddled mounts standing at the racks with drooping heads.

And there were no people.

Sitting Carter Willis's chestnut mare, he folded his hands on the saddlehorn and took a long look around. No, he wasn't mistaken.

The place was deserted.

As the thought formed, he paused, cocking his head. *He had heard singing — distant singing, group singing . . . a hymn.*

'‘Rock Of Ages’,' he murmured and looked for the church.

The street lifted in a low rise at the northern end and he saw the small grey building with the peaked, red roof, and a small steeple at one end. Then he saw the crowd of people, gathered beneath some trees, a moving blur, at this distance.

It was a funeral. There were gravestones visible beyond the gathering: the local Boot Hill . . .

Then, behind him, across the street, he heard the sounds of breaking glass. He hipped quickly in the saddle, hand dropping to the butt of his Colt. The sound came from the only brick building in town: the *Federation County Bank*.

As he watched, the double, half-glass front doors were kicked open and three men ran out with canvas sacks in hands, one man also carrying a leather valise.

They headed for the hitch rack where four horses waited. They slung the bags over saddlehorns, the valise, too, hanging by its handle, and struggled to swing up into leather.

The red-haired one, bushy moustache matching the lank hair showing under his hat, saw the man with the dead men draped over his second horse.

'*Hell!*'

The others swivelled their heads as they mounted and then all three were reaching for their guns. The man-hunter's Colt whispered out of leather and barked three times. Two of the bank robbers were punched from their saddles, one lying on his side, head resting on an outstretched arm, resting: but his rest would last for eternity.

The other downed one writhed in the dust, knees drawn up to his chest.

The redhead was unscathed, fought his prancing mount, throwing down with a couple of wild shots as the horse wheeled and began to lunge away.

The man-hunter was stretched out along the mare's back now, and he slid to the ground, using his free hand to slap the mount's flank. It pranced away with a snort and, on one knee, he crooked his left arm, rested the warm gun barrel across it, and beaded the fleeing robber. The gun bucked and the redhead was punched to one side, where he clung precariously to the saddlehorn, trying to heave himself onboard again.

But he had been hit and he lost his grip and struck the street rolling and bouncing. He skidded and slewed into the gutter and lay there. By the time the man-hunter stood over him, Colt reloaded, Red was sitting up, dazed, face gravel-scarred and bleeding, his left arm hanging uselessly, shoulder bloody.

'You . . . sonuvabitch! Where'd you come from . . . ?'

The man leaned down, fisted up some greasy cloth of the robber's shirt and heaved him to his feet. Red roared in pain, his right hand whipping up to press at the bleeding wound in his shoulder, trying to staunch the blood.

As he was dragged back towards the bank and the two men lying on the street — the wounded one still now — folk came hurrying back from Boot Hill. Most were on foot and running, but some had taken time to mount their horses, while still others had piled into buggies and buckboards, all eager to see what the shooting was about.

Red was dumped unceremoniously against a hitch rail post where he sat, hangdog, mouth open, eyes pain-glazed. A man with silver hair and who looked like a sawbones — and was — knelt with a small black bag open on the ground beside him and began to examine the wounded robbers. Some folk crowded around to watch.

There was no need for explanations: the townsfolk could see exactly what had happened.

Which drew full attention to the man-hunter standing hipshot, buttocks against the hickory rail, the bloody robber at his feet.

A big man with thinning white hair and blotchy face, wearing a good quality dark-grey suit, stepped forward. 'Who might you be, sir? I mean, we know the wounded man at your feet is Red Higgins, a no-good layabout, who seems to have out-classed himself by trying to rob our bank while we were away, but it's obvious you are the saviour of our money, and we would like to know *your* name. *I*, by the way, am Carson Ivers, *Judge* Carson Ivers, Circuit-Court Judge and also Mayor of Hopeful — '

'An' a talker like you wouldn't believe!' called someone in the crowd, getting a laugh. 'Give him a chance to answer, Judge!'

Ivers smiled sheepishly, made a slight bow. 'My weakness is oratory, sir. We await your name . . . '

'Catamount Cody, Judge, but mostly I get Cat.'

That name brought a brief silence, not because it was known to anyone there, but because it was unusual.

'You hunt cougars, Mr Cody?' Ivers ventured.

'Cougars, grizz, jaguar, buffalo, snow wolf . . . '

'A mountain man!' someone opined.

'Er, which mountain, sir? There aren't any really high ones close around here worth a trapline.'

'Little ways north; you care to name any mountain and most likely, I've run a trapline on it sometime or other.'

The crowd digested this, then a tall, broad man in his late twenties, some years younger than Cody, stepped forward. There was a tin star pinned to his black vest.

'I'm Blake Ross, sheriff here — '

'Er, acting sheriff, if you please, Blake,' corrected Judge Ivers and earned himself a scowl from Ross which didn't seem to bother the judge. 'You haven't yet been appointed.'

Ross turned his scowl on Cody. 'What the hell happened here, Cody?'

'See for yourself. I rode in, town was deserted, then these three come a-busting out of the bank carrying money sacks. They saw me and started shooting.'

'And you shot back?'

'I'm no walking target, *Acting* Sheriff.' Cody looked levelly at Ross, his eyes hard and challenging, and it seemed to throw the brash young lawman.

'Well — I mean — most men with

three hardcases shootin' at 'em would've ducked for cover.'

'They didn't give me time.'

'You're saying you had no choice but to shoot back?' Judge Ivers remarked but Cody didn't make any sort of reply.

'Damn glad he did!' spoke up a middle-aged man in the front of the crowd. 'He saved us our money!' He walked forward, right hand outstretched. It was a hard, firm hand as Cody found out when they gripped. 'Jim Crane, storekeeper and town councillor. My personal thanks, Mr Cody.'

Cody nodded, looked around at the animated folk. They were all dressed in their best for the funeral.

'You folks must've been burying someone popular, the whole town deserted the way it was.'

Judge Ivers' fat, bewhiskered face, sobered. 'Aye — our late sheriff, Nate Palmer. A fine lawman who kept our tolerably new town on the straight and narrow and had the respect and high regard of everyone.' He sighed heavily.

'He went down to the county seat at Federation to marry the young love of his life. Unfortunately, he was murdered in cold blood and his wife was . . . violated and hanged down the trail at a place called The Crossing — hereafter, forever known to our town as *Devil's Crossing*. Three other passengers, guard and driver, were also killed.'

'Hard luck,' Cody allowed, frowning. 'They get the men who did it?'

'Not yet. One of the passengers had a heart attack and was left for dead, but he lived long enough to tell us it was an outlaw named Arnie Kelsey.'

Cody nodded slowly. 'Seen his dodger in a few places.'

'Make a note of the bounty on him?' asked Blake Ross curtly, drawing attention now.

'What's that mean, Blake?' demanded Jim Crane.

Ross, with a crooked smile on his rugged, not unhandsome face, jerked a thumb towards Cody's horse with the two bodies draped across it.

'I reckon we've got us a bounty hunter here — that right, Mr Cody?'

'Not even close, Ross. Those two were men who committed a crime way down in Bowie County.'

'With bounties on 'em!' insisted Ross.

'That I dunno for sure. Reckon there might be and if there is, I aim to collect.' His eyes were pinpoints of tempered steel now.

'Like I said, just a damn bounty hunter who happened to have enough luck to down them bank robbers!'

'He saved our money, Ross,' a tall, beanpole of a man standing beside Jim Crane said, his tobacco-stained frontier moustache bristling. 'I got no objections to rewardin' him.'

He looked around, tall enough to stand half a head higher than anyone close by, and there were murmurs of approval.

Except Blake Ross — he scowled again. 'Sure, Larrabee. Throw a few bucks his way, then he can quit before fillin' our streets with any more dead men.'

'Be glad he did, Blake. You must've had your money in the bank, too.'

Ross flushed. 'Never did trust banks.'

Someone laughed. 'Well, you hear that? Our big-note sheriff-elect don't even have a bank account! No wonder he expects so many free drinks in my saloon!'

'What the hell difference does it make? I'm still the best man for the sheriff's job! I don't have to be rich — Nate Palmer left me in charge while he went off an' got hitched and now he ain't coming back so that makes me — '

Judge Ivers suddenly turned to Cody. 'Perhaps we could reward you in some other way than cash, Mr Cody?'

Cody frowned. 'Well, I'm in need of money, Judge.'

'You could have it regularly. Say, two-hundred a month, and perhaps some sort of arrangement for each arrest . . . ?'

There was silence in the hot street, until an outraged Blake Ross said,

'Dammit! You ain't offering him the *sheriff's* job!'

'Well, of course, it would have to be discussed fully at a council meeting — which is scheduled for tonight, by the way — but I believe Hopeful would benefit from a lawman who has demonstrated his . . . prowess as well as Mr Cody has. What d'you think, folks?'

There was a lot of loud talk and discussion, even jostling with some of the men who got a mite heated, and then there was a gunshot that brought everything to a standstill.

As the echoes of the single shot died away, the townsfolk all stared at the smoking pistol in Cody's hand.

'Mebbe someone ought to ask me if I'm interested.'

The crowd shuffled a little. There was some murmuring. More than one man had his ribs poked by his spouse's elbow, urging him to speak up.

But it was the judge who asked, eventually, 'Well, Mr Cody, please consider yourself asked. We'd be delighted to welcome you as our new sheriff — at a salary yet to be negotiated.'

Cody's gaze rested on Blake Ross. The man was pale and tense, his jaw jutting. One big hand opened and closed on the holster that held his six-gun.

Smiling faintly, Cody said slowly, 'Well, that's mighty fine of you folks to offer, and I'd like to accept — '

There was instant murmuring and fast talking, even a faint cheer or two — and a murderous look on Ross's face. Cody's thin smile widened as he added, watching the man, 'But like *Acting* Sheriff Ross inferred, I'm only interested in the money right now. Pay me the bounty on these two men I brought in and I'll be on my way.'

'See?' Ross said loudly so he could be heard over the new burst of animation. 'Told you he was nothin' but a lousy bounty hunter!'

3

Who's Next?

It was easy to see that Sheriff Nate Palmer was going to be missed. The standard of the funeral and the quality of the marble headstone told that plainly enough, and the entire town turning out for the graveside service.

As for poor Ellie, his wife, well, she was an outsider, not from around Hopeful, although she did reside in Federation County. No one was too sure how Palmer had come to meet such a young, beautiful and essentially fragile woman but if he had chosen her to share the rest of his life, it was OK by the town.

Not that they weren't disappointed the wedding hadn't taken place in Hopeful, but they understood that Ellie had wanted it in Federation because her father was an invalid there and unable to travel far.

But now both were laid away on Hopeful's Boot Hill and there was a need for a new lawman.

Deputy Blake Ross was experienced but he had had to be held in by Palmer many a time. Ross was brash and arrogant, fancied himself as a ladies' man, and a bit of a brawler. He looked for opportunities to prove this on any occasion that offered: he was certain sure he would automatically be given the sheriff's badge after Palmer's death. But Judge Ivers had dashed that hope, *and* in front of the whole goddamn town to boot! So Ross turned his resentment upon Cody. It was not the man-hunter's doing, of course, in fact he had refused the job, adding that he would be happy to go after Arnie Kelsey and his pard if there were bounties to collect.

This was a point raised by some town councillors, including Pru Riordan, the only female member. She owned Block

R, the biggest ranch in the county, having inherited it when her father had been backshot by rustlers.

'My father helped build this county, sank a lot of money into the roadworks for the town, donated the church and the school,' she told them in her usual feisty manner, when she had first applied for council appointment. 'He is no longer here and no one can say he wasn't a damn good council member. So, as his only surviving kin, I am putting myself up for membership. And fully expect to be accepted.'

There was great consternation among the male councillors and the judge had argued strongly to reject the application. But Prudence Riordan had not accepted the rejection: she turned up on Ivers' doorstep one night about supper-time and the judge and his wife found they had no alternative but to set an extra place at the dining-table.

It was a pleasant enough meal and afterward, in the judge's smoking-room

31

— where Pru lit a long slim cheroot — the ranch woman began a seemingly casual conversation about the county and how it was growing fast, and how many of the now prosperous business folk owed their success to old Brock Riordan not calling in his notes on money he had loaned them so they could get started.

Although she was still smiling, and looked handsomer than ever in her lavender-frilled dress, chestnut hair coiffured to pefection, Judge Ivers felt that old trembling jump in his belly that meant *trouble is a-brewing!*

'Pa knew how hard it is to start a business from scratch in a town that hasn't yet established itself. Did you know he started out as a feed-store owner on borrowed money? Way back in the early days of Tucson?'

'No, I did not know that.' Despite himself the judge answered curtly.

'Oh, yes, he almost went broke twice and by then he had started a family so he took one more gamble — on the

cattle business. You know how successful he was at first, a trailherder and later
a cattle agent for the meathouses, and
finally the most successful rancher this
county is ever likely to see.'

'Yes, my dear, he certainly was that,
but — '

'He always told me that there should
be a Riordan on this town council, if
only to watch over his . . . investments.'

'His — ? Is that what he called his
loans?'

'What else could you call them,
Judge? He invested in the future of
Hopeful, even suggested the town name
if you recall . . . ? Yes, of course, you do.
Actually, it was I who suggested the
name to him and he passed it along as
being his own idea, for even then he
realized there would be reservations
about accepting any suggestion from a
woman.'

Judge Ivers tried to wave that aspect
away, but only wafted the thick smoke
from his cigar into his face and caused
a fit of coughing.

'You know the prejudice is there, Judge, don't try to deny it. I know it, too, and I am prepared to stand up for my rights.'

'Rights!' blustered Ivers. 'My dear girl, the only *rights* a woman has is the right to bear her husband's children and to be subservient to his wishes.'

He felt that quivering deep in his belly once more at the slow, knowing smile she gave him, the hazel eyes crinkling at the corners. *He had fallen into her trap!*

'You are way behind the times, my dear Judge! I'll bring you some of the latest thinking concerning women's rights in several recent pamphlets issued by *The Independent Woman's League.* You've heard of it, of course?'

Ivers spluttered. 'By Godfrey I have! But that's all right those hussies beating their breasts — pardon, Pru — their *bosoms* in New York. This is different out here.'

'I'm not offended if you say 'breasts', Judge. They are the mark of a mature woman. I'm quite proud of mine . . . '

She squared her shoulders, thrust out her prominent breasts — a mature woman, indeed, and not yet in her thirties. The judge looked away hastily: this was moving into territory he had no wish to be in. He cleared his throat noisily.

'I believe we will leave things right there, Prudence.'

That faint disconcerting smile again. 'Oh, I think not, Judge.' She stood and started for the door. 'Why don't we ask your wife to join us and see what she thinks?'

'All *right*! Oh, damn you and your free-thinking! I will ever be surprised that old Brock actually encouraged it. He was, of course, without the guidance of your poor departed mother's hand but — '

'I had a fine upbringing, Judge, as you well know. I can run Block R as well as any man, work right alongside my cowhands and do as good or better job. Just what did you mean when you said 'All *right!*'? Am I to take it that you will recommend my membership to the town council?'

The judge knew when he was beaten: this was the best — the *only* — way of avoiding massive embarrassment and confrontation, not only for himself, but the other council members.

So Pru Riordan joined the council. And now she had her say in the present discussion: should they appoint Catamount Cody as Sheriff of Hopeful over Blake Ross?

A vote was taken and there was a majority wanting to offer Cody the position again, even though he had already refused it. One of the dissenters was Pru Riordan.

'I'm not *for* Blake Ross particularly, but this Cody is hungry for blood money,' she explained briefly when Ivers braced her about it. 'Not the kind of sheriff our town needs.'

'He's *definitely* the kind of sheriff we need, Pru. Look how he tackled those bank robbers, all on his lonesome.'

'No doubt hoping to collect bounty on them, too.'

The judge left it at that: no male member of the council cared for long discussions with Pru Riordan when it was clear she had already made up her mind about something.

When Ivers spoke to Cody later, he pointed out that it might be a few weeks before the bounties on Carter Willis and Ed Curtin were approved, or even ascertained if there were bounties payable.

Cody frowned, paused with his cigarette halfway to his lips. 'Now that seems a strange thing to say, Judge.'

Ivers moved uncomfortably. 'Perhaps, but the fact is — well, Blake Ross has been unable to locate any wanted dodgers on Ed Curtin or this Carter Willis. I believe I saw them both on my rounds when I was doing the Circuit Court once, but it was for a trivial matter.'

Cody smiled thinly, then drew on his cigarette. 'I'm with you now, Judge. But

I've seen dodgers on 'em, down in Bowie County. Never took much notice at the time, only after we had our . . . difficulty. Pretty sure there was a good-size bounty on each.'

'I'm sure Nate Palmer would have been up to date with all current Wanted dodgers in circulation, Cody.' He let it hang, and Cody nodded slowly.

'I guess so, from what I know about Palmer. Think I'll have a word with Deputy Ross.'

'Wait! Er . . . Blake's quite upset as it is, not getting the sheriff's job as he expected, it might be best to wait a while and — '

Cody crushed out his cigarette under his boot. 'I can't wait forever, Judge, I need that money. I'll go see if I can help Ross out . . . mebbe he only needs reading-glasses.'

Ivers groaned a little to himself as the tall man-hunter straightened his hat and strode across the street and entered the law office.

Blake Ross had been watching from

the front window and was just easing down into his chair, when Cody entered.

'What d'you want?'

'Figured I'd lend you a hand going through that pile of dodgers. You don't seem to've found any on Curtin or Willis.'

Blake Ross smiled, eyes mocking. 'That's because there ain't any. You got some questions to answer, mister, luggin' in a coupla dead men who don't seem to've been doin' anythin' agin the law.'

Cody stepped forward, picked up the three-inch pile of ragged dodgers and hurriedly shuffled through them. 'You're right, no dodgers there I'm interested in.'

Ross's smile widened. 'So, mebbe you better explain just how come you arrive with two dead men you admit you shot?'

'Mebbe I'll explain sometime, but not to you. I smell something burning.' Cody was on his way around the desk moving towards a door leading into the small yard behind the law office as he spoke. Blake came out of his chair as Cody wrenched the door open.

Smoke rose from a wire waste-basket a few feet outside the door, a few flames flickering. Cody tipped out the smouldering ashes, stamped out the remaining fire. Ross, face stony, stood in the doorway as the bounty hunter picked up some of the charred and crumbling remains. There were no words visible, but the heavy paper was definitely of the kind used for Wanted dodgers.

'Them's some old, out-of-date dodgers. Fellers've either been caught, already in jail, or Boot Hill.'

Cody flicked his steely gaze to the big deputy's coarse features, thinking, irrelevantly, that they were the kind of looks that would appeal to some women.

'You're fibbin', Blake!'

Ross came ramrod-erect, eyes blazing, hand whipping to his gun butt. 'You callin' me a liar?'

Cody hadn't moved. 'Was bein' polite, but — yeah, guess it comes down to me calling you a liar.'

'By God!' Ross started his draw, halted, jaw sagging as he looked down the barrel of Cody's Colt, rock-steady in his fist. He gulped as the man shook his head slightly.

'You don't want it to come to a gunfight, Ross — or maybe you do. But I'm here to tell you, you're a dead man right now if I let this hammer spur slide from under my thumb.'

Blake Ross was white now, lips bloodless. He opened his fingers and eased his hand out from his side, away from the gun butt.

After his breathing settled some he said, hoarsely, 'So — you — you're a gunslinger, too!' He gave a brief laugh. 'You got a lot of explainin' to do to the council! They won't hire no gunfighter and I'll see you never get your hands on that bounty.'

He realized he had said just a mite too much as Cody smiled thinly. 'What bounty would that be, Ross?' He indicated the charred remains near his scuffed boot. 'The one you said don't exist?'

Ross licked his lips. 'There's nothin' you can read in them ashes!' He managed a smile of triumph. 'So you'll never know, will you?'

Cody's face scared Ross for a moment but he had little time to think about it. Cody grabbed his arm, jostled him roughly back into the office, bouncing him off the wall until they reached the front door. Then he heaved violently and Ross yelled as he stumbled wildly across the narrow landing, hit the rail and jack-knifed over to land in the street.

Judge Ivers had been just coming up the short row of steps and stopped in his tracks. He looked sharply at Cody who still had his Colt in his hand.

'That snake burned the dodgers on Curtin and Willis.'

Ivers, aware folk were gathering now, spoke sharply to Ross who was getting to his feet, dusting down his clothes. 'Is that correct, Blake?'

'Hell, no! They was old dodgers, on men already put away or dead, is all.'

'I see — who?'

Ross blinked, hesitated too long, tightened his lips and swore, pointing at Cody. 'He's a gunslinger! Ought've seen the way he got that Colt out! He's a professional — an' he threatened me, said he'd kill me!' He raked his gaze around the gawking crowd. 'He ain't what this town needs for a sheriff!'

He let his triumph reflect in his flushed face as the crowd discussed this accusation. Ivers frowned.

'I'm fairly quick on the draw, Judge,' Cody told him quietly. 'But I'm no gunslinger. This idiot's just slower than a fly in molasses — makes me seem like greased lightning.'

'By hell, you've made enough fun of me, Cody!'

And Ross did a brave — or a foolish — thing. He lunged at Cody, ignoring the man's gun, swung a looping punch. It caught Cody on the edge of the jaw, snapped his head violently to the side. He staggered and managed to holster the Colt as the deputy stormed after him, hands clenched into fists big as a horse's hoof.

Judge Ivers shouted for them to stop, but it was a half-hearted bellow: most townsfolk would like to see Big Blake Ross taken down a peg or two. Not that it looked like happening here right now, mind.

Ross bulled his way after Cody, using his big body to keep him off balance until Cody brought up against the landing in front of the law office. Then Ross set his big boots, tree-trunk legs solid and spread, as he loosed off a barrage of blows. Cody ducked and weaved, covering as well as he could. Some blows got past his darting guard and slammed against his head like hammers.

Lights streaked and burst behind his eyes. He tasted blood. His nose was driven to one side and hot blood coursed over his upper lip and dripped from his chin. He was cramped by Ross's body keeping him pressed back against the raised landing. Risking a bunch of rock-hard knuckles taking him squarely in the face, Cody straightened, got his feet set and kicked Ross between the spread legs.

The deputy gagged and gasped, twisted away, swaying and dancing as he tried to stay on his feet, doubled over. Cody stepped after him, drove a fist into the man's kidneys, then chopped a blow into the side of the thick neck. Ross was driven to his knees, breath still hissing between his big yellow teeth as snakes of pain twisted and writhed through his belly. He suddenly roared, shoulders heaving, startling Cody, as he lunged up awkwardly, baring his teeth with effort.

Cody instantly slammed him in the midriff and Ross sagged. The man-hunter set his feet, got his right fist back behind his hip and pivoted. His whole body was behind the blow he drove against Ross's square jaw. The man's hair flew out from his head with the impact and the deputy's eyes rolled upwards, showing white. He collapsed in a slow spiral, not moving once he hit the dust.

There was silence, a drawn-out silence, broken only by Cody's ragged breathing, his chest heaving.

As the talk began, Judge Ivers stepped forward tentatively. 'That is the first time anyone has knocked down Blake Ross, let alone fought him to a stand still!'

'Should be more of it!' a burly man yelled, grinning. Someone cheered and it was taken up by a couple of dozen other voices.

'We'll take Cody for sheriff, any time!' someone bawled and others agreed.

Judge Ivers was frowning, looking thoughtful as Cody wet his neckerchief in the horse trough and began mopping his blood-streaked face.

'I'm not so sure about this — I think it will have to be put to a council vote.'

'You old fogies can vote all you want,' a man bawled. 'Ask the townsfolk! We're the ones know the kinda man we want wearin' the sheriff's star! Cody's the man for us!'

A hundred voices lifted in agreement.

4

Blood Money

Judge Ivers had started the process of finding out whether there were, in fact, bounties on Ed Curtin and Carter Willis by forwarding Cody's claim to the county office in Federation.

But the county would need to get in touch with the states or territories that first posted any such bounties.

And that would take time, even by telegraph.

'You could earn yourself a few dollars while you wait, by taking the sheriff's star, Mr Cody,' coerced Judge Ivers. 'I — er — can arrange free accommodation for you and perhaps even free meals, although I'm not certain about that last.'

'How long, Judge?'

'Well, in my experience, these people

are never in too much of a hurry to pay over bounty monies, most of which were posted by folk in the heat of the moment, enraged by some misdeed of the outlaws. They cool down after a while and wish they'd kept their mouths shut.'

'I've dealt with folk like that before, Judge. I waited a month once. I won't wait that long this time.'

Ivers frowned. 'You do seem to be in quite a hurry . . . ' He paused hoping for confirmation, or, better still, an explanation, but Cody merely waited in sober silence. 'I'll see what I can do, Mr Cody. I'm sure if they knew you were about to accept a lawman's badge . . . '

Cody nodded, a hardness in his eyes that unsettled the judge even more. 'Yeah, I see where you're going with this. I'll wait it out because I *do* want the money, Judge. Now, there's a lot of talk around town about what folk would like to do to this Arnie Kelsey and his bunch for the massacre at Devil's Crossing. I've had a few hints that mebbe I should go after those killers and avenge your sheriff — because the posse from Federation seem to have given up. Kelsey needs killing, Judge, I'll grant that, but if I go after him, I can't do it for nothing.'

He let it hang. Ivers tightened his lips. 'Well, I guess I hoped you might be a mite less . . . mercenary, but this possibility was discussed at the council meeting, and we decided the town would put up a bounty for the capture of Kelsey, or any of his gang, dead or alive.'

'Which means 'dead'.'

'Er, yes, I suppose so. We'll offer a bounty of one thousand dollars.'

Cody waited and when Ivers didn't say any more, added, 'Each.'

The judge blinked. 'I-I don't know. There were three of them, one of whom was killed by Kelsey. We've already spent — '

'This town can afford two thousand dollars for the men who killed Nate Palmer, Judge. This is a prosperous

50

town and set to prosper even more when the trail herds begin passing through here on the way to the railhead at Federation.'

'You know of this?'

'I keep my ears open. The sheriff's job'll be no pushover then, Judge. But when I come back to collect my bounties, I'll take your sheriff's badge if the job's still open.'

Ivers blotted sweat from his face with a cream silk kerchief and nodded jerkily. 'It'll still be open . . . but we will stipulate a minimum time for you to remain in the sheriff's office.'

'Ross'll be wanting to take it on.'

'Of course, but Blake is good deputy material, no more than that, and he is nowhere near as popular as he thinks. Nor as tough, apparently, after he — er — tangled with you.'

'Mebbe I was showing off a little, but the man grates on me.'

'He grates on *everyone*. Have we a deal? You take the badge for — say, six months?'

Cody thrust out his right hand, and Ivers gripped with him. 'I'll have the agreement drawn up and — '

'We just shook on it, Judge. That's good enough for me.'

'Of course.' Then the judge smiled. 'Perhaps we could seal it — officially — with a drink?'

Lightly tugging at a loosened tooth in his swollen gums, Cody removed his hand from his face and smiled.

'No need to twist my arm, Judge. Lead the way.'

★   ★   ★

Leaving the judge's Main Street offices, Cody saw a familiar silver-haired man hurrying towards him.

'Mr Cody — I'm Dr Timmins. I've tended to Red Higgins and he's fit enough to — er — reside in a cell now.'

'What about his sidekick?'

Timmins pursed his lips and shook his head briefly. 'His injuries are more serious. But to be honest, Higgins is fitter than he lets on and I'm worried he might break out of my infirmary.'

'OK, Doc — I'll take him down to the jailhouse for you.'

Timmins heaved a sigh. 'Thank you very much! He's a hardcase and has beat-up several men. Nate Palmer had him in jail two or three times.'

Cody found the bank robber manacled to the bed and Timmins had the key. Red glared as Cody unlocked the chain. His left arm was in a sling.

'You the sonuver who shot me!'

'And I'll shoot you again, you got any notion of making trouble. Grab your hat, Red.'

Higgins curled a lip, but when Cody lifted his Colt he complied readily enough. 'I coulda been rich, if it wasn't for you.'

'We all have our dreams, Red.'

During the short distance to the jail, Higgins began to breathe hard and stagger. 'Hell! Weaker'n I figured.'

'You're going to jail, Red — walking, crawlin', or being dragged. Up to you.'

Cody shoved the wounded man roughly, watched curiously by several passers-by.

Blake Ross wasn't pleased to see Higgins, snapped his head up from where he sat behind his desk. 'The hell's this?'

'Prisoner. Doc Timmins asked me to bring him in.'

'Well, he can go to hell — I ain't gonna nursemaid no bank robber.'

'Take it up with the sawbones. He's all yours.'

Cody shoved Red roughly into a chair and the man groaned, blood draining from his face as he grasped at his wounded shoulder. Blake was still swearing and shouting when Cody went outside again.

Ross glared at the sullen Higgins. 'Would've been better if Cody had killed you during the hold-up.'

'Not for me! You better take good care of me, Ross!'

'Why? 'Cause you're hurtin'?' Blake Ross's face took on hard lines. He reached over and grabbed Higgins by the wounded shoulder. The man yelled and writhed, slid out of the chair to huddle on the floor, moaning.

Ross came round the desk and stood over him, nudging with his boot. 'Get up! You try anythin' and I'll shoot you, Red.'

Higgins struggled to a sitting position, face blanched and lined with pain. 'Gimme a . . . hand.'

He reached up but the deputy slapped it aside, folded his arms and watched Higgins grunt and gasp his way back into the chair.

'Wh-why you doin' this to . . . me?'

Ross snorted, dragged the protesting man out of the office and threw him roughly into a cell. As he locked the door, Red crawled on to the bunk, glaring.

'At least gimme somethin' to eat.'

'Supper's at sundown. Now shut up.'

'I think I'm gonna kill you, Ross!'

'Lots of luck!'

★ ★ ★

Judge Ivers had arranged for a free room for Cody at the smaller of Hopeful's two hotels, the Midway.

He was stretched out on top of the bed covers, having a last cigarette before turning in, when there were excited voices out in the passage, followed by an urgent hammering on his door.

'Mr Cody! Mr Cody! Are you awake, sir?'

When he wrenched open the door, a wild-eyed desk clerk from the foyer stood there, hopping from one foot to the other in his excitement. He stepped back when Cody appeared.

'Oh! Sir, I'm sorry if I woke you but there's been a breakout from the jail! Red Higgins is on the loose and Judge Ivers told me to fetch you and — '

He was talking to empty space.

Cody ran to the bed, hurriedly pulled on his boots and snatched his gun rig from where he had hung it over the back of the bedside chair. He buckled it on as he hurried to the top of the stairs as gunfire crackled from down in the street. When he reached the boardwalk, Colt in hand, he saw people running and a commotion near the livery. Someone called his name and he turned towards the jail.

Judge Ivers was there, steadying Blake Ross who had blood running down his face from a cut above his hairline.

'What happened?'

'Higgins. I was takin' him supper. Grabbed my six-gun and slugged me . . . Gone! Took my horse from the stable behind the jail . . . '

Cody started towards the livery where people were milling about and horses, too. He heard Ross say,

'Dammit, Judge! I don't want Cody in this!'

'You'll need all the help — '

Ross shoved the judge aside roughly, lurched back into the office. When he stumbled out again, he had jammed on a hat with a folded kerchief over the head wound and held a rifle.

'Blake, you're being foolish! Cody and you can form a posse and — '

'Cody can stay out of it!' snapped Ross, blinking, obviously feeling the effects of the blow on the head. 'All of you stay out of it! Higgins is my responsibility and I'll bring him back.'

'You'll kill yourself!' Ivers snapped, looking around at the gathering crowd. 'Come on! Some of you younger men! Grab your guns and help Blake out!'

There was more discussion and argument, but Cody rode past on his chestnut mare and that was all Ross was going to take. Floundering some, he slammed a way through the people and snatched the reins of a mount from the nearest man, and, with a grunting leap, was in the saddle, rifle held out to the side in one hand, spurring away.

'Judas priest!' the horse's owner yelled, starting a few steps after Ross. 'Take it easy, for Chris'sakes! It ain't used to spurs . . . '

Within minutes there were four more mounted men heading out of town, including the popular Jim Crane from the general store. Jim was always willing to help where he figured he could — and this included deliberately making mistakes in his additions on orders for folk he knew were struggling to keep food on the table, or needed a warmer shirt, or had children whose boots were worn through.

He was a lanky man and a good shot, although he always said he could never shoot down another human being.

'Even an animal, I'd balk before pullin' the trigger,' he admitted on more than one occasion.

The rest of the posse was made up of townsmen: none really qualified to go up against a hardcase like Red Higgins, but having a sense of 'duty' and so wavering consciences had tugged successfully — if not exactly willingly.

Cody had taken the only way out of town at the north end, over the narrow bridge across the creek that cut Main, with only a hide tannery beyond. He smelled the hides and the tanning pools as the mare clattered over the wooden bridge and then he slowed, waiting for the others to catch up.

Ross had swung away on his own and Cody hauled rein, saying to Jim Crane, 'Where's he likely to go? Not much use just riding around in the dark.'

'Red has kinfolk in the forest. Likely to make for them. Follow me, Mr Cody.'

Cody did, and the other men drew back a little, losing some of the first heat of enthusiasm now the lights of town were falling behind — and remembering their warm beds and women were back there.

Gunfire echoed from ahead and Cody could make out the flashes of at least two guns. He swung that way, cutting off Crane who hauled rein hurriedly, swearing. Then the store-keeper spurred after Cody, fumbling to make sure his pistol was still in leather.

There were more shots and Cody figured they had come from within the first line of trees. He saw movement to his right, turned the mare that way, his Colt in hand. It was Blake Ross, reeling in the saddle. Cody called out to ask if he had been hit.

'No! Damn head's . . . spinnin'. You ain't s'posed to be here, Cody! This is my deal!'

'You got any sense, you'll stay back. Way you're staggering all over the countryside, you'll run into a bullet.'

'I said you ain't wanted!'

Cody wheeled away, hearing a horse crashing through trees, the swish of branches marking a path.

He had excellent night vision from tracking animals in the mountains in all kinds of light and weather. So he saw Red Higgins's mount plunging through the trees, weaving, Red lying low in the saddle. He hauled the mare left and then forward, aiming to cut Red's path. It meant a lot of dodging, lying low with his face buried in the horse's mane, branches scraping his back: if he rose even an inch he would be in danger of having his head smashed in.

Higgins hauled rein, sawing wildly with the bit, stopping his mount just in time from crashing into a clump of trees that were much closer together than he had been riding through. The sweating horse whinnied in protest and half-reared.

Red swore, fighting the reins, lost his balance and fell. The horse ran off and, panicking now, Higgins lunged up just as Jim Crane came thundering in: he had seen Red, too, and, like Cody, aimed to cut him off. But he knew the forest better than Cody and had arrived first.

He skidded his mount to a halt and pulled his gun.

'Give up, Red! There're too many of us!'

'Not right now, there ain't!' Red brought up his gun, shooting as he threw himself to one side.

The bullet missed and his hammer fell on an empty chamber when he triggered again. Jim Crane had ducked and, a man not used to a lot of riding, started to slip from the saddle. Red jumped forward, grabbed the storekeeper by the collar of his shirt and heaved. Crane was flung roughly to the ground, hit his head on a root and sat up, dazed, blinking.

Red was in the saddle of Crane's horse now and fought it with savage wrenches on the reins, set it plunging forward as the storekeeper staggered up, trying to bring his gun around. The horse whinnied as it instinctively leapt forward, smashing into Crane, driving him down underfoot. Its hoofs stomped and scrabbled for purchase and then Higgins was riding away from the blood-spattered form of the storekeeper sprawled unmoving on the ground.

When Cody crashed out of the trees, his face bleeding from where low-swinging branches had raked him, he saw Red, brought up his Colt and fired two swift shots. His horse lunged at the same time and the lead missed Higgins — but slammed into his mount. It went down, trumpeting, nose first, ploughing up a carpet of dead leaves and other forest detritus.

Higgins yelled as he was thrown out of leather and crashed into a tree trunk. He fell unconscious.

Cody was kneeling beside Crane when the others rode up, Blake Ross the last man. 'Who's that?' the deputy demanded.

One of the townsmen lifted a pale face. 'It's Jim Crane! That bastard Higgins done rode him down with his own hoss! Aw, hell, Jim's all smashed up!'

The man jumped up, looking round wildly, saw Red's dark form lying at the base of the tree and ran across with an anguished cry and started to kick him. Cody leaned down from the saddle and hauled him off.

'Leave him.'

'That — that son of a *bitch*! Jim Crane was a decent man! Only practisin' Christian I've ever knowed! He treated my family good — you others an' your families, too! Now he's gonna die or end up a cripple, 'cause of this lousy — '

'Higgins needs stringin'-up!' someone spoke up, but Cody fired a shot into the air, drawing their attention instantly. 'An' I mean now!'

'None of that! Higgins is knocked out. Get him back to town and locked-up proper this time.' His eyes sought Ross: the big deputy's face was streaked with drying blood. 'He's your prisoner, Ross.'

'Yeah! An' don't you forget it. Would've saved a lot of trouble and the expense of a trial if you'd shot Red instead of the hoss!'

'Well, he's all yours again — and you're gonna have to put down any talk of lynching, right away.'

'Don't try to tell me my job, dammit! I know what to do!'

Cody nodded. 'Reckon you do. Someone better make a travois for Jim and get him back to Doc Timmins. If Red needs the sawbones, he can see him in the cells.'

'Damn you, Cody! I'm the deputy here! You ain't nothin' but a lousy bounty hunter right now. I don't need you! You'd do best to pull up stakes.'

'Know what, Ross? I think you could be right. So maybe I'll just do that.'

5

Bounty Trail

Next day, word came through that there were bounties available on Curtin and Willis, payable by Bowie County: $3,250 would be deposited into the Federal Bank at Hopeful, to the credit of Wesley C. Cody, upon acceptable identification of the bodies.

Judge Ivers had seen the bodies when Cody had first arrived. He recognized both men, having had them before him a year earlier, on a charge of drunken brawling, causing damage and injury, in one of his courts which he conducted all over the territory in his capacity as Circuit Court Judge.

'I'm satisfied they were Ed Curtin and Carter Willis, Cody. I've sent a wire off to Bowie County to that effect. You should be able to draw your money in a few days.'

'Obliged, Judge.' Cody was standing beside a new mount, a bay gelding, and a pack horse, supplied, a mite reluctantly, by the town council. He was just outside the gateway to the livery stables' corral, and reached into his shirt pocket, handed Ivers a folded piece of paper. 'When the money's through, Judge, will you ask the banker to keep a hundred dollars aside for my use and send the rest to this address?'

The judge instinctively read the address. 'A law firm in Denver? I thought you were from down south, somewhere.'

'I'm from all over, Judge. Will you do that? And ask the banker not to waste any time.'

Ivers nodded as he put the paper in his pocket, looking curiously at Cody. 'It's none of my business, of course, but . . . '

Cody swung up into the saddle. 'Thanks again, Judge.' He paused, then said, 'Higgins is a damn fool. Hope

Ross can handle it. If Jim Crane dies, I'll bet my boots you'll have a lynch mob on your hands.'

'By God, I hope you're wrong!'

'Me, too. *Adios*, Judge.'

Judge Ivers looked worried as Cody rode off: he wished Cody was already wearing the sheriff's badge.

* * *

It was a long ride down to Devil's Crossing. Cody didn't expect to find much that could help him, but Arnie Kelsey had smashed the wheels of the stage after he and Dack were through and there were people working on it who might know something.

The wheelwright in Federation had had to make a full set of replacement wheels and a work team had been sent out to fit them so the stage could be returned to town. Cody figured some of the men might have been in the posse from Federation and he was right. There were seven men working to get the stage roadworthy again and three of them had ridden with the original posse.

Cody introduced himself, adding, 'Heard you quit early.' He knew it would likely stir them up, but hoped that in their anger they would tell him exactly what they *had* done before turning back, trying to justify their quitting.

A man named Morton glowered: he worked for the stage company in Federation and resented Cody's remarks.

He sniffed, rubbed grit and sawdust out of his bushy moustache and side whiskers, squinting.

'We didn't aim to ride into no head shot, *that's* why we give up! Sam Reeder followed some tracks by his lonesome and we found him shot in the back. We got him to town and the posse disbanded — see? We wasn't bein' paid no bounty! They never came up with one till after we was back in town and — well, we all got wives an' kids, and not a one wanted us to go back after them road-agents. Not chasin' someone like Kelsey after Sam was bush-whacked.'

Cody nodded. 'I can savvy that. Like you to tell me where your friend was drygulched and you turned back.'

Morton spat. 'I don't have to help you.'

'No, you don't, but you gotta think that mebbe your wife and kids could be on the next stage Kelsey decides to hit.'

The men murmured and Morton flushed. 'And helpin' you claim your blood money'll prevent that?'

'If I'm lucky enough to get the jump on Kelsey.'

Morton snorted, turning to look at the others. 'You hear that? *Lucky* enough, he says! We had twenty men in that posse and now this sad son of a bitch is gonna get *lucky* an' bring back Arnie Kelsey!'

A man near Morton said in a careful voice, 'He's the one shot up Red Higgins's bunch when they tried to rob the Hopeful Bank, Mort.'

That brought a frown to Morton's face. 'That right?'

'I got lucky,' Cody said, with a crooked smile. 'Just like I did with Ed Curtin and Carter Willis — thought I might as well make it three in a row with Kelsey.'

'Well — hell! I din't know that . . . but I still don't like bounty hunters.'

'You got plenty of company. Now, you gonna help me or not?' Cody's voice was cold and impatient now.

Morton squinted again. 'I don't like someone tryin' to push me around, neither.'

'I climb down and start *pushing*, you'll know it. C'mon, Morton. Time's wasting. Kelsey's had a damn good start and he left a lot of good men dead. I've got a decent ordnance map in my saddle-bags, how about you show me where you quit?'

Morton didn't like giving in but the others told Cody to get out the map and they would try to find the place where they had turned back.

Once the map was spread out on a

rock and coffee had been brewed and passed around, Morton tended to take over again. He was corrected two or three times by others who had been on the posse. Cody was surprised that he could actually see hills they indicated, right now, where the townsman was bushwhacked. It was hazed by distance, but rose to a good height against the blazing sky.

'Hell, you didn't get very far!'

The men looked a little sheepish. 'Seems the stage had a load of bonded whiskey on board, bound for some rich rancher. Them killers took it and had themselves a wingding in the hills — drank it dry. We wasn't expectin' to catch up with 'em so soon.'

Cody swore. 'Twenty men! And you *still* couldn't take them? Even drunk or nursing hangovers?' He shook his head unbelievingly. 'To top it off, you rode smack into their ambush! Mighty careless, fellers!'

Morton bristled. 'We ain't professional man-killers with a heap of blood money waitin' for us to collect!'

'You ain't professional anything, sure not trackers. Mebbe you know your trades but you're no good on a posse chasin' cold-blooded murderers like Kelsey.' Cody paused. 'No, I guess that's unfair. You men volunteer because you figure it's what you should do to help protect your families and your town — and it is — whether you got the know-how or not. That's why posses always lose a lot of good men, I guess . . . But there's another thing.' He looked around as they stared at him expectantly, tight-faced after his criticism. 'It's possible Kelsey could have his hideout somewhere in those hills. Might still be there — maybe not yet sober, but primed for another massacre if he sees the chance.'

It was obviously something they hadn't thought of and most of them glanced involuntarily towards the range in question.

'Be a good spot, at that!' one bearded man said, tugging at the lobe of half an ear: the rest had been sliced by a piece of shattered blade in the sawmill years ago. 'A good pair of field-glasses, watch and pick the stages they want to hit soon as they see there's a shotgun guard on board — '

'Which would mean the stage is carryin' a strongbox!' chimed in another, with an edge of excitement, nodding vigorously.

Another man gave an involuntary shiver. 'Judas! I been huntin' in them hills with my eldest boy lots of times!'

Cody tossed out the dregs of his coffee, rinsed the mug and pushed it back into his bedroll. He swung into the saddle, settled, and took the folded map Morton handed him.

'I can see you're pretty good at this man-huntin' thing, Cody. Guess I'm a mite sorry I missed out on a bounty.'

'I'll be more than a mite sorry if *I* miss out. Obliged for your help, fellers. See you on the way back.'

One of them called after him as he rode off, the pack horse trailing, 'We'll look for a rider leadin' a hoss with a coupla bodies over it.'

The others backed him up and Cody smiled slightly.

''Long as I'm the rider.'

He lifted a hand and rode on. They were surprised when he suddenly swung left, slanting away from the hills.

'Now where the hell's he goin'?'

'Mort, if there's a chance Arnie Kelsey is waitin' in them hills, would you want him to see you comin' straight for him . . . ?'

Morton grunted. 'Well, best take a good look at Cody. He aims to tangle with Kelsey on his own stampin' ground — you won't see him again this side of Hell.'

* * *

Cody had misjudged the range of hills: they were a lot further off than they had seemed, shimmering in the heat-haze.

He had hoped to make a long swing away from them and, at sundown, turn back towards the hills and make a fast night ride, arriving before daylight.

But the land was misleading. What had seemed like flat prairie from Devil's Crossing was pocked with buffalo wallows and deeper depressions from past floods, most of these with eroded washes snaking in many directions. It hadn't taken him long to lose his orientation, for some of the gulches were deep enough to cut off his view of the hills, and they twisted and writhed like a ball of yarn after a kitten had finished playing with it.

When he finally found a way out, he was facing in the wrong direction.

Then sundown came, and it filled these washways and draws with deep shadow, which was fine for covering his movements, but only as long as he didn't stray out on to the plains, still ablaze with sundown fire which lasted for almost another hour.

He was trapped in the hollows and, making the best of a bad situation, he set up a cold-camp, ate hardtack washed down with water. There was a patch of grass for his horses and he short-hobbled them so they wouldn't stray from the shadowed draws.

Cody was mad at himself, specially after criticizing the posse men and their lack of man-hunting ability. But there was little he could do now until the sun dropped behind the range. He lit a cigarette, smoking it cupped in his hand: he knew just how far a cigarette end or the flare of a match could be seen in the dark across the prairie.

The sun went down and the scattered, writhing long shadows melded: as if the entire prairie had shrugged on a cloak of darkness. He got the horses ready and when it was black enough, stars blazing in a cloudless and, thankfully, moonless, sky, he rode up and out of the imprisoning draw.

The range was a thick, notched black bulk across the horizon and he rode that way as fast as he dared. A horse's leg finding a prairie-dog burrow would be disastrous at this stage.

He no longer approached the range

at a tangent, but rode straight towards the huge bulk looming across the stars. It was dangerous riding, but he wanted to be well within those foothills before any sign of approaching daylight.

His original plan had been to reach the hills right after dark: it was usually easier to see the first flare of a camp-fire as the evening meal was prepared. Later it would be allowed to burn down to coals and, while these, too, would be visible, they were not as reliable as a fire with flames and rising sparks.

But, by the time he was in the foothills, anyone hiding out here — and he was not certain Kelsey was here, of course — would have turned in and either let the fire burn down, or banked the coals behind rocks to conceal them.

Both he and the horses were in need of rest. He found a dry wash with brush along the edges where he bedded down, sleeping with both rifle and six-gun under his blanket.

He awoke to gunfire.

It was barely light down here on the

slope where he had slept. But higher up, the sunlight was strong, painting the crest of the range with glowing gold, paling to yellow as the sun climbed higher.

It was from up there that the gunfire was coming from. Properly awake now, he grabbed his Colt, holstered it and lifted his Winchester as he stood up, eyes and ears straining. *One — two — a dead second or two, then three.*

Well, it sure wasn't a gunfight. More like someone deliberately shooting — maybe at a stationary target. No animal he had ever hunted would stay still long enough to give the shooter that much time to draw a bead.

The gunfire continued, desultory, sometimes with a gap of as much as twenty seconds, other times, three or four rapid shots.

Whatever the explanation, it had to be investigated.

Cody saddled his mount and the pack horse, but decided to leave the latter. He lengthened the hobbles a little so it could find its way to the creek further along the gulch, then mounted and rode out cautiously, rifle butt on his right thigh, a cartridge in the breech.

The light was still greyish down here but shortly he was riding in strengthening sunlight, weaving a way up the slope, keeping to whatever cover he could; a small field of boulders, canted as if ready to roll to the bottom; some brush, scraggy and not very tall, but useful. He worked into a fold between the hills, having sorted out the rolling echoes of the gunfire, pinpointing it to a ridge the dark shadow of which hung a hundred feet above him.

It would be too dangerous to ride all the way up: he could easily be spotted, and a man with a gun and the advantage of possessing the high ground would have an easy target. So he dismounted behind a large, egg-shaped boulder, anchoring the mare's reins with a head-sized stone, and started up on foot.

The shooting had diminished now — reloading, maybe? — but he had picked his landmarks and still knew where it had originated. Sweat ran down his face, soaked his collar and armpits. The slope angle steepened and he had to slip the rifle barrel through his belt so he could use both hands and boots to climb one section.

Breathing hard, he pulled himself over a broken, narrow ledge and sat back against a shale wall, listening to his heart hammering in his chest as he freed his rifle from the belt.

'Bet you're Cody.'

He jumped at the sound of the raspy voice — like a harsh whisper — still holding his rifle awkwardly after he had eased it from his belt.

He saw a broad, stubbled face grinning at him over a sawn-off shotgun, a large gap in the front teeth.

'Only a mountain man could make it up a steep slope like this fast as you did.'

Cody smiled faintly. 'You're right. I'm Cody and I'm looking for . . . ' He flipped the rifle suddenly as he spoke, and the weapon spun end-over-end, the brass butt plate taking the outlaw lookout just above the eye. The man slid sideways, jarred off balance more by surprise than hurt, although there was a trickle of blood. He put down a hand to keep his balance, loosening his grip on the shotgun. As he tried to firm it again, Cody launched himself and drove the point of his shoulder against the man's jaw. He fell, the shotgun clattering and skidding off the ledge now, to Cody's relief. He rammed in, hooking with a left, knocking the man into a small crevice. As he drove forward, the outlaw swung up his boots, caught Cody's hip and spun him into the rock.

Cody clawed to keep from tumbling over the edge and the outlaw came out of the crevice in a rush, knotted fists sledging. Cody's boot skidded and one leg folded under him, saving him from a crunching blow that would have smashed his nose through to the back of his head. It struck his shoulder with enough force to knock him side-on to his adversary and another fist took him in the lower ribs, bringing a grunt of pain from him as he doubled over.

The outlaw brought up a knee and it thudded into Cody's forehead, straightening him abruptly. The other man was too eager, lunged from too far away, his lashing blow missing by an inch. Cody, acting by instinct, head throbbing, ducked, came up inside the man's guard, rammed the top of his head up under the square jaw. He heard the big teeth click together and the outlaw stumbled back, spitting blood.

Cody's left hooked him on the jaw, swiftly followed by another left just under the right eye. He set himself and his arms worked like pistons as he hammered the thick body from midriff to throat. He stepped quickly forward as the man staggered towards the edge. It began to crumble under his weight and Cody bared his teeth, swung a rounding kick into the back of the man's thighs. His legs went out from under him and then he was spilling head first off the narrow ledge.

He hit hard and bounced across a flat rock, skidding off to drop to the gravelly slope. Limply, the body slid and tumbled, finally stopping, against a tree stump. He would be out of things for quite some time.

Cody sat down, breath rasping, body and head sore from the punishment he had taken.

Then the desultory shooting commenced again, high above.

One thing he was mighty grateful for: it had been a silent fight. No yelling, no guns — whoever was up above obviously didn't know there was an intruder.

With a little luck, he could still find his way into Kelsey's hideout.

Whether that was a good or bad thing he didn't know.

But he was about to find out.

He picked up his rifle, set his hat on firmly and started up the rest of the slope.

6

Target

Sweat-soaked, fingers and leg muscles aching, heart thundering, lying there in the grass just below the ridge crest, Cody saw he had been right in one supposition: the man doing the shooting was aiming at targets.

The targets were bottles — lines of empty whiskey bottles. He figured they would be the ones from the cases of whiskey stolen from the stage. *Hell, these fools must have been drunk for days!*

And they must have full confidence in the location of their hideout — sure did not expect anyone to find it because of a little gunfire.

Then again, if their brains were pickled day after day in good, strong whiskey, they may not have even given thought to possible discovery.

But there had been a lookout.

And there had also been the fool who had decided to get in some target practice — and wake up the whole county.

There he was below, reloading a smoking pistol, swaying, feet sliding a few inches this way and that so he could keep his balance. The line of empty bottles — the wavering line — was about thirty feet away. A few had been shattered and shards of dark-brown glass caught the sunlight and threw it around the hollow of the campsite behind the man.

There was a corral with horses, and two cabins, rough as cobs, but adequate in warm weather at least. Cody wouldn't care to be living in one of them when the blizzards hit. There was a man down there, outside the cabin closest to the trail that wound down the slope, sloshing water from a cut-down beer keg over his head, soaking his shirt.

Even as Cody watched he leaned a shaky arm against the corner of the cabin, pushed lank hair back from his dripping face and yelled, 'Will you cut out that goddamn *shootin'!*'

He quickly grabbed his head in both hands, hawking as he started up the path past the rickety outhouse to where the other man stood, his pistol reloaded now.

'Sorry, Arnie,' the target-shooter slurred. 'Din' mean to wake you.'

'You dumb bastard! You think shootin' rotgut bottles is — is — *quiet!*'

Arnie Kelsey snatched at the other's gun, but the man pulled the weapon out of reach. He held up a hand to ward off Kelsey's second try for the Colt.

'S'all right for you, Arn, you're a good shot. I ain't. Took me three tries before I finished that banker's wife . . . jus' tryin' to improve meself.'

Arnie Kesley squinted at Dack Jameson. 'Huh? Ah, you're still drunk.'

'So . . . you!'

'Me? Well, mebbe . . . just a l'il.' He held up a hand, thumb and tip of forefinger about an inch apart. Then he grinned owlishly. 'OK! S'all gone now, the 'skey. We berrer sober up — go find somewhere to spend that loot . . . buy us some women, 's'well as 'skey.'

'I'm all for that . . . But lemme take another crack at them bo'les, Arn. Know I can hit 'em.'

Kelsey took Dack by the shoulders, turned him and started to push him forward. 'Get closer — You can't hit the side of a barn with a six-gun this far off . . . '

'Aaah! Tha's the trouble!' Dack laughed harshly. 'I thought it was me! An' all the time it's them crazy bottles marchin' away from me.'

'OK. This is good enough. We'll line 'em up on that pile of dirt with the cutbank behind — an' we'll see who's the best shot.'

'Aw, ha! What you wanna bet?'

Arnie laughed. 'Bo'le of whiskey?'

They both guffawed and were trying

not to stumble when Cody stood up and worked the rifle in four fast shots.

Four whiskey bottles shattered, glass flying wildly and Dack sat down in shock. Arnie Kelsey was bent almost double and squinted as Cody came forward.

'Jesus! Who you . . . ?'

'I'm a better shot than either of you, fellers. You want to lift your hands? Higher — grab a really big handful of that sky — that's it. Now you might's well drop your guns, you won't be needing 'em from here on in.'

'You neither,' said a voice behind Cody and he started to spin around, but there was an explosion of light.

Then nothing.

★ ★ ★

When he came round, he was bound hand and foot with rawhide thongs — and lying against a sloping bank of earth. Dirt and stones had worked inside his shirt collar and rubbed the back of his neck raw as he moved. He grunted, opened his eyes — carefully — for his head was pounding. He felt like a goose-egg was growing out of his forehead. And he was right: the flesh was bruised, cut and swollen.

Through half-open lids he was startled to see a row of empty bottles lined-up about five or six feet in front of him. Two had broken necks but the others seemed to be intact.

Opening his aching eyes more, he could even read an oval label: *Turkeyshoot Bourbon*. He realized where he was then: hogtied *behind* the target bottles Dack Jameson had been shooting at.

Only now the bottles were lined up neatly enough on an old plank — and he was between them and the earthen bank that had been absorbing Dack's bullets.

He saw Arnie Kelsey and Dack Jameson loading their Colts. Dack looked up, saw Cody was awake and nudged Arnie, grinning.

'He's with us again.' His words

weren't so slurred now but he swayed some, so that meant a good deal of alcohol was still swirling through his veins — and whatever he used for a brain.

Kelsey squinted, not looking too spry, and Cody figured the booze was likely wearing off and the onset of a hangover was not to Arnie's liking.

'Uh-huh. Then we can get started.' Kelsey raised his voice as he closed the loading gate of the revolver. 'You comfy, Cody?'

'Wouldn't mind sitting on that log down there by the first cabin for a spell.'

Arnie guffawed and Dack grinned. 'Funny man, ain't he? Well, you gonna sit where y'are for a spell — while we practise shootin' them bottles. You feel up to it, you might want to dodge an' weave a little . . . '

'A damn lot, I reckon!'

'Mmmm — could be. Well, we'll see. Who goes first, Dack? Wanna flip a coin?'

'Aw, age before beauty, they says, so . . . ' He made a sweeping motion with his left arm, bowing stiffly — and almost overbalanced. He swayed wildly as he straightened. 'Whooo! Somebody hold the world still, pul-eeasse!'

Kelsey smiled crookedly. 'Yeah. Could do with a steadier meself . . . '

He was lining up his Colt, sighting as it moved slowly along the line of bottles. Suddenly, he stopped.

'Hey! They only twenny-three bottles!'

Dack blinked. 'Well, that's enough, ain't it? The way we shoot — '

'You dumb Reb! We took two cases of 'skey from the stage. *Two* — that makes twenny-*four* bottles!'

Dack shrugged. 'Musta shot better'n I figured.'

'The hell you did! You've hardly touched 'em.' Kelsey, frowning now, mouth drawn tight, turned towards the second cabin down the slope. 'Git on down there, see what Gumbo's doin'.'

'He said he's gonna wash-up. Cody beat the hell outa him an' then that climb back up the slope, so's he could jump Cody, muddied him some . . . '

'*Get down there!* The sonuver's took a bottle for hisself! Must've stashed it away when we got back from the Crossin'.'

Dack swore and started weaving down the slope. Arnie watched for a moment, turned to look at the trussed-up Cody.

'You gonna be a long time dyin', feller — them bullets'll cut you to pieces before you croak.'

'Aw, might get lucky and stop one in the ticker.'

Kelsey snorted derisively. 'You ain't all that funny, you know? See, we gonna start at the ends and work our way back to the middle of the line — by the time we get there, you'll be sittin' in a pool of your own blood.'

Cody didn't reply: the damned sadist was likely right!

There was some yelling from the cabin. Then Gumbo, the lookout with the big teeth who had fought with Cody on the ledge, staggered out and almost fell. Dack Jameson stepped after him, Colt in one hand, holding a bottle by the neck in the other. He held it up.

'You was right, Arnie, he had one stashed. Still three-parts full.'

'I aim to get the same way. Bring it up here.'

'What about Gumbo?'

'Aw, Arnie, I din' think you'd be riled!' Gumbo called, and there was an edge of fear in his voice. 'I was just gonna take it with me up on the peak for night lookout — gets mighty cold up there and — '

'You sneaky sumbitch!' yelled Kelsey and his Colt swept up and bucked twice in his hand.

Startled, Dack jumped back inside the cabin, as Gumbo was punched backwards by the two bullets. His legs folded and he clutched at his chest, looking up-slope to Kelsey with accusing eyes. Then he fell forward on his face.

Sniffing, Arnie punched out the smoking brass cases and replaced them with cartridges from his belt loops while Dack hurried up.

'Hell! Nothin' wrong with your shootin', Arn!' He held out the whiskey bottle and Cody could see his arm trembled a little.

Kelsey was a scary character, all right.

'Yeah — s'prised meself.' Kelsey rammed his gun into his holster, snatched the bottle from Dack and took a deep draught, afterwards smacking his lips. Dack reached for the whiskey, but Kelsey pulled it out of reach and drank again.

'Hey!'

'All right, all right. Here. An' don't drink it all.'

As Dack took the bottle, Arnie spun towards the line of bottles, his Colt coming up, blazing in a roar of rapid shots.

Two bottles shattered, glass flying, making Cody wince as shards ripped his shirt sleeve and sliced his flesh. He jerked his head instinctively to one side as Arnie's bullets punched into the earthen slope he rested against.

He wondered how long he would last . . .

While Kelsey reloaded, Dack, having had his drink, set the bottle down carefully on the ground and lifted his gun. He sighted owlishly, the barrel wavering, got off three shots, ragged spaces between as he cocked the hammer. The neck flew off one bottle and he whooped like a Comanche, as it toppled off the plank.

Kelsey scowled. 'Go set up the damn bottle again.'

He took another long swig from the whiskey and Dack looked at him sullenly when he returned, snatching the bottle from him as Arnie sighted on the targets again. He only hit one this time but it was dead centre and glass flew in all directions, a curved piece half as big as the palm of a man's hand landing between Cody's legs. His breath hissed out slowly and the outlaws laughed.

'Don't worry, Cody, you won't be needin' that tackle again!' Kelsey said, laughing.

They fought for the bottle now and it looked like turning nasty but Big Arnie prevailed and, sullen and angry, Dack emptied his gun at the bottles. He missed every one, and Cody, who had thrown himself sideways, looked up slowly, spitting dirt.

Arnie was laughing, lifting the whiskey bottle for another swig, and then there was a gunshot — from down the slope. The bottle shattered in his hand, whiskey spraying.

They spun towards the sound and Cody stretched up to see who was doing the shooting. It was Gumbo, bad-hit, but trying to take at least one of the others with him when he finally died. *Tough man, surviving that fall off the ridge and Kelsey's bullet . . .*

Kelsey and Jameson dropped flat, Dack hurriedly reloading now. Arnie fired, and swore bitterly as a shot from below flicked his upper left arm. He threw himself to one side, away from Dack, rolling. Jameson, reloaded now, jumped up and started to run for a log they had been trimming for firewood that lay at one end of the line of target bottles.

He didn't get far: Gumbo's next shot took him in the spine. Cody heard it crack as the man arched like a drawn bow and collapsed over the log, head and arms on one side, legs pointing down the slope.

Arnie Kelsey was up and running now and he triggered twice at the prone, wounded Gumbo. His lead tore a line of dirt to one side and Gumbo ducked his head, but wasn't hit. He rested his elbows on the ground, holding the Colt in two blood-sticky hands, beading Arnie.

Seeing this, Kelsey dived for cover, rolling behind a pile of split wood near the first cabin. He fired rapidly at Gumbo, more to throw the man's aim than with any real hope of hitting him, then hunkered low, reloading with shaking hands.

And while this was taking place, Cody, trying to heave himself around and get closer to the log where Dack hung lifelessly, so he would be safe from stray lead, felt his hand touch the large shard of glass that had landed between his legs.

His fingers closed over it convulsively and he grunted as the flesh was sliced and started bleeding. But he held on to the glass and, half-sitting now, worked it edge-on up between his hands. He began to saw at the rawhide thongs that bound his wrists, cutting himself, blood flowing and making the glass slippery, but continuing, teeth gritted.

Arnie was now reloaded and Gumbo tried his last shot as the man raised up behind the pile of firewood. Splinters flew and Kelsey, rising more, grinned: he knew Gumbo's gun was empty now, and he took his time beading the exhausted, dying man, then fired three spaced shots into him, the last finding Gumbo's head.

Kelsey's grin was tight as he walked

forward, kicked Gumbo in the side and toed him on to his back. He knelt and started to go through the man's pockets for any money he might have — and there was a nice clasp knife with a polished horn handle he had always fancied . . .

Then a gun crashed and a bullet burned air past his left ear. Startled, he reacted by instinct, threw himself forward across Gumbo's body, twisting so he landed on his back, Colt seeking a target.

He jerked his head and grunted aloud in surprise when he saw Cody kneeling by the log with Dack Jameson's body draped across it. The man's hands were dripping blood but they held Dack's six-gun and, even as Arnie Kelsey absorbed this, flame stabbed from the gun's muzzle.

He was knocked back by the bullet searing across his chest, and returned fire by instinct, wasting lead. Cody ducked and Arnie leapt up, weaving his way towards the cabin, shooting under one arm.

Cody, leaning across Dack's still warm body, steadied his arm, fired three evenly spaced shots. Kelsey was propelled viciously by the impact of the lead. He was flung hard against the cabin, just short of the door, twisting, mouth hanging, and blood already spilling over his lips. As he jarred on to his knees he got off one final shot —

Cody's head jerked, hair flying upward and out as he was flung back, blood coursing down his wolfish face.

7

The Singing Hills

Pru Riordan was dressed very differently to when she came to Hopeful for a town council meeting.

Instead of the mail-order dresses from some of the East's most expensive stores, she was wearing range clothes — checked shirt, denim work pants, high-heeled boots that had done as much walking as resting in the stirrups, judging by the looks of the worn heels — and a wide-brimmed hat with a leather tie thong under her jaw. She carried a quirt as she made her way down to Doc Timmins's infirmary.

In the small room outside the main infirmary the sawbones was writing in a ledger when the nurse showed Pru in. He smiled. 'Straight in from the range, I see.'

'Yes. We were working along our southern line searching for mavericks and I decided to ride into town, pick up a few things and see how Jim Crane is doing.'

The medico pursed his lips and shook his head, a worried frown between his eyes. 'Not very well, I'm afraid. If the good wishes of everyone who's asked after him or who've stopped by to see him, were medicine, he'd be out of here and back behind his store counter before you could snap your fingers.'

Pru frowned slightly. 'I suppose that's your way of saying that there doesn't seem to be much hope for him.'

The sawbones tightened his lips a little and nodded curtly; he ought to have known Pru Riordan wouldn't appreciate his attempt at lightening bad news.

'He's very badly hurt. At least seven ribs smashed and I'm sure his lungs have been penetrated. His chest is caved in, restricting his heartbeat. His skull is fractured where a hoof struck it.

His own mother wouldn't recognize him: that same hoof skidded right across his face . . . '

Pru held up a hand. 'That's enough, Doctor. No need to be too graphic.' Her frown deepened. 'How long do you think he'll . . . last?'

'He'll be dead by morning, if there's a merciful God. I've given him as much opium as I dare and he still cries out in terrible pain. I can't administer any more — too big a risk of slowing his breathing to the critical stage.'

'Red Higgins has a lot to answer for!'

'That's one of the things that worries me, Pru. If Jim does survive, he'll be a cripple, maybe mentally deficient, certainly he'll have internal troubles that will plague him. That's why I say it would be a mercy if he died while the opium has him in its grip. You can imagine how folk'll react to Jim Crane being a cripple, barely alive.'

'And if he dies, the town will explode!'

'Without a doubt. There isn't a more

popular and respected man in Hopeful than Jim Crane. If he dies, it'll be murder, but these law-abiding citizens are going to want Higgins's blood much sooner than if he goes to trial.'

'Does Judge Ivers know how bad Jim is?'

'Yes, and he's also afraid we may have a lynch mob on our hands.'

'I've been thinking about that, too. Is Blake Ross good enough to handle such a situation?'

The medic gave her a steady look. 'You know he's not. I've already spoken to the judge about it and he agrees — we're hoping Cody will get back before it happens.'

'Cody! He's still off chasing blood money on Arnie Kelsey and Dack Jameson, I suppose.'

'Whatever he's doing, he isn't here.'

'Well, someone will have to do some straight talking to Blake Ross, make him see he'll have to deputize some help!'

'Who do you think will accept a deputy's badge, even if Blake would agree to offer it, from amongst our townsmen? To prevent Jim Crane's killer from getting his just desserts? I doubt you'd find a single taker.'

Pru coloured a little at the medic's tone, but nodded jerkily. 'Yes — you're right.'

'Even if Cody were here, he might not be able to do anything. We have good people here, but that's part of the problem: it takes a lot to stir genuine rage in peaceful folk, but when it happens . . . ' His lips compressed. 'It can be far worse than just a drunken mob on a rampage.'

'Well, I doubt that Cody will be here to help. He's obsessed with his blood money. We can't rely on his returning in time. But . . . I may be able to help. I can bring in half a dozen of my best men and the judge can deputize them and . . . '

She let her words trail off as she saw his face.

'My God! Surely you're not in favour of a *lynching!*'

He sighed and shook his head, looking a mite sheepish now that he was aware his inner emotions had been on display, even fleetingly. 'No, of course not, but I could almost forget my Hippocratic Oath in this case, Pru! I've tried to treat those massive injuries and — I'm only human — I could almost bring myself to kill the man who caused them with my bare hands. But you're right. Mob rule can't be tolerated. Perhaps you could have your men keep an eye out for Cody? He must be working over towards your range, or in that general direction. It's said those Singing-Stone Hills near your boundary is where Kelsey has his hideout.'

'So they say. We've searched a few times when he's rustled some of my stock but never found a trace of him. I'll have my crew keep a lookout for Cody, but I think I'll bring some men into town just the same. They can be here by nightfall. They'll be on hand if — when the worst happens to poor

Jim.' She sighed, adding quietly, 'But, like you, Doctor, I'm tempted to just let the mob rule. Red Higgins will be no loss to the world.'

★　★　★

When Blake Ross pushed the coffee mug through the bars and Higgins took it, one-handed — his shoulder wound stiffening now — he met the deputy's steady gaze.

'You should've let me get away.'

'You think so? You think it wasn't bad enough that you slugged me and stole my horse for your escape? How you think that made me look?'

Red shrugged, sipping the coffee.

'No, you wouldn't even know what I'm talking about!'

'You worry too much about what people think of you.'

'Dammit, I want to be sheriff of this town! I can make it mine and it'll be a lot better'n it is now — full of damn Bible-bangers and Sunday Go-to-Meetin's!'

'You'll have them same folk kickin' down your goddamn door if Crane dies — to get at *me!*'

'More fool you for ridin' him down! Christ, the most popular man in town! They'll have you danglin' from the end of a rope ten minutes after he dies!'

'Well, it don't have to be that way: you could fix things so I get outa here before Crane croaks.'

Ross snorted and turned away from the cell door. 'You're plumb loco, Red! The town won't stand for that.'

Higgins tossed what was left of his coffee through the bars and some splashed on the deputy's boots. Blake Ross's mouth tightened.

'Mebbe I could make it worth your while: I got a little stashed away.'

'Keep your 'little'. You stay put.'

Red was up against the bars now. 'You throw me to the mob, Ross, and I'll yell my head off before they get the noose around my neck!'

Ross smiled thinly. 'You think they'll give you time to say anything? No one'll

110

be listenin', Red. All they'll want to do is drag you out kickin' and screamin' and lynch you — there's a couple of likely branches on that big elm over the water trough, almost opposite.' Ross strode away, laughing. 'You won't last long, Red. Lie there and think about it. Or go to sleep.' As he reached the door at the end of the passage, he called out, 'Pleasant dreams!'

'I'll fix your wagon, see if I don't! I know plenty about you, Ross, you lousy *bastard!*'

The door crashed shut, echoing down the passage to Red Higgins's cell like the crack of Doom.

* ★ *

The Singing-Stone Hills were a phenomen in Federation County — the only county in the south-west that could boast anything like them.

One of the ranges seemed to be all black — basalt and lava rock, sparse vegetation. But underneath the many

111

black rocks, varying from fist-sized to house-sized, were myriad volcanic tunnels. Strike one of these rocks, anything larger than a pine-slatted store crate, and there was a hollow, booming sound that, as it rippled away through connecting rocks and the tunnels, rose in cadence to a high-note ringing that took minutes to fade.

The strange thing was that while the rocks rang when struck by almost anything solid, it was only when they were struck with a rock of similar material that the best result was obtained. Folk who had heard it, with the wind just right and blowing mournfully through the tunnels and laval-pipes, claimed it was like a carillon, sweeter and more enduring than any originating in a Boston cathedral.

It was said that some men had tried shooting at these rocks known to give off the 'singing' tones only to be disappointed to find the lead bullet did no more than leave a grey streak across the black surface.

Indians claimed the sounds were made by the spirits of the dead, for, over the years, many men, women and children, keen to explore the tunnels easily accessed between the boulders, simply disappeared.

No one who had entered had ever returned, not even those who swore they would only explore for a few yards.

It was a sacred place to the Indians and there were enough superstitious whites living in the area to give the Singing-Stone Hills a wide berth.

Which made the place an ideal hideout for men who were on the dodge.

Catamount Cody hadn't realized Arnie Kelsey's hideout was just over the rise from the singing hills. But he found out when he worked his chestnut mare up the slope, leading the pack horse with Kelsey's dead body roped across it. He had covered Dack Jameson and Gumbo with rocks as well as he could but the head wound was giving him lots of trouble: he kept fading away into sleep and once fell completely out of the saddle.

It took him almost half a day before he could mount again. Luckily it happened on a patch of grass which kept the horses close by and cushioned his fall at the same time. He had lost a good deal of blood, not only from the head wound, which he had covered with folded bandannas taken from the dead outlaws and wadded in place with his hat, but also from the many cuts from the shattered glass. His sleeves were soaked and his body had collected more cuts from flying glass. He had even self-inflicted some on hands and wrists while cutting himself free.

When the horse took him over the crest and walked its way down the other side, carefully, through the reddish haze that seemed to be a constant companion now, he saw the Singing-Stones.

He had heard of them and seen them once before, a long time back before Hopeful had been built. He had been on his way north to the snow-capped Rockies for a season of bear hunting and trapping beaver and snow fox. In a brief moment of clarity he recognized them now but didn't figure they could aid him in any way.

The horses for some reason were heading towards them, and though he tried to turn the mare she picked a way through some of the black rocks, ignoring his pressure on the reins. He was too weak to pull her around by brute force. The pack horse followed.

Then he recalled the *Well of Purity* as the Indians had named a rock pool, sheltered by overhanging rocks, water so clear it didn't seem to even be there until it was ruffled by a breeze or a waterbeetle. The Indians believed it gave a warrior strength — and lent its power to his horse just before battle.

The truth was it contained some mineral, unidentiftied as yet — something from deep in the bowels of the earth — and horses liked it. The liquid itself was cold, not icy enough to make man or animal recoil, but chilled to a pleasant degree that slaked even a massive thirst, and for a long time.

Some instnct had brought the mare here and she and the pack horse slurped at the pool while Cody, hit by yet another dizzy spell, clung to the saddlehorn and tried to keep from falling.

He snatched wildly as he felt himself going, steadied, but the sudden shift in weight pulled the mare away and she cannoned into the pack horse. It whinnied and snorted and snapped, its load sliding a little. Both horses seemed off balance now and crashed into a pile of rocks: Cody just managed to save himself a crushed leg by pulling it free of the stirrup in time. But he fell against the rocks and in his efforts to keep from falling, grabbed wildly at the teetering stack.

He knocked several rocks from the pile and it collapsed, spilling them over the slope, rolling off the ledge to patter down on the big black boulder beneath.

Seven rocks, five as big as a man's head, crashed on to the big hollow rock below. Then a dozen smaller ones.

Even as Cody toppled to the ground, with lights swirling and exploding behind his eyes, he heard the booming, ringing, singing, as the sound transmitted itself through the entire length of the hillside.

The strange sound carried far on the hot air.

★ ★ ★

Chip Garner crashed his mount with the leather chest protector through the prickly brush. He cursed as the maverick that had been hiding there, suddenly erupted, lowered its head and raked a horn tip across his leg before smashing its own path out of the thicket.

He was wearing leather chaps which took the brunt of the lunge, but it still hurt his leg and almost unhorsed him. The bay plunged and rolled its eyes in fright and Chip reared back too high in

117

the saddle: a low branch knocked off his hat and banged his forehead, spilling him in a flailing heap.

The horse plunged on a little way, calmed down after its years of training in brush-popping, and stood with lowered head while Garner sat up, blinking.

His head was ringing and he had a large red welt across his forehead. The skin hadn't broken but he was groggy when he recovered his bashed-in hat and had to set it on the back of his head. It hurt too much to put it on in the normal manner.

He mounted again — after three tries — dropped into the saddle like a bag of bricks, bringing another snort from the bay. He could still hear the maverick crashing away on its own path and he thought, To hell with it! He wheeled the gelding and made his way back out of the thicket.

He came out on the almost bare slope below the brush and scrub, stopped by a convenient rock and stepped on to it. He let the horse wander a few feet with trailing reins while he rolled a cigarette with trembling fingers. As he lit up he shook his head.

Man! His skull was ringing from that damn branch!

He jammed a grimy finger into each ear, wiggling them, trying to get rid of the annoying ringing. Halfway through his cigarette it was still there, undiminished, and he frowned, sat up straighter, then stood and looked around.

Along the face of the slope he could see the blackness of one end of the Singing-Stone Hills. He licked his dry lips. *By God! The ringing wasn't in his head! It was coming from that pile of black rocks everyone at Block R told him was jinxed.*

Chip was young and sceptical, used to having pranks played on him and being told tall tales just because he had a baby face, and was essentially a greenhorn as far as ranch work was concerned. The older hands simply couldn't resist putting him through the hoops.

Well, seemed like the tale about these rocks ringing and singing under certain conditions wasn't such a tall one after all . . .

He ground out the cigarette under his boot, still a little groggy, then walked across to the bay and mounted by standing on a rock so he wouldn't have to strain so much getting back into leather.

The bay was settled now and made no protest as he lifted the reins and touched his spurs to its flanks, heading towards the Singing-Stones to see for himself what made them boom and ring like that.

Maybe he'd have his own tall tale to tell when he got back to the bunkhouse tonight.

He'd try it first on Pru — for some reason she had taken a shine to him, kind of protected him somewhat from the worst of the seasoned crew's pranks. Someone said it was because he reminded her of her kid brother who'd drowned years earlier, but no one gave him the full details of that so he reckoned they were joshing him once more.

'Well!' he said aloud, urging the bay on faster. 'Pru ought to be interested, even if the others make fun of me.'

8

Fire on the Mountain

How could he feel so damn hot when he was wading through snow? It didn't make sense: but then, not much else did, either, right now. What was he doing back on the mountain?

He smelled smoke before he saw the black rolling clouds smearing the sky near the crest. He was plodding through the snow cap, crotch-deep, dragging the floundering pack burro reluctantly after him, the roped-on pile of pelts sagging to one side. Cody knew he would soon have to stop long enough to settle them squarely, or the animal would dig in and refuse to move, or toss the lot off.

He was about to halt when his nostrils twitched with the tang of woodsmoke. He knew instinctively it wasn't from the cabin's chimney: these days, Old Trapper Jack preferred his grub mostly raw — he wouldn't bother lighting a cooking fire while Cody was away.

That was when he first saw the roiling smoke and knew there was more than just a cooking fire up there. He whipped out his hunting knife and cut the straps holding the pelts on the pack mule. They spilled down the slope and the animal brayed with pleasure at relief from the load.

By then Cody was plunging on through the snow, rifle in hand, floundering in his hurry, leg muscles screaming, arms thrown outward for balance. He spat snow from a freezing mouth after falling several times, moved to the fringes away from the deeper drifts and made better time.

As soon as he got to the crest, heart hammering, breath roaring, he tightened his grip on the rifle and started to run as well as he could in his heavy furs.

The cabin was ablaze, well and truly. The hide racks had been smashed, the hides gone, even the pegged-out ones that hadn't yet been salted-down.

'Jack! Jaaacckkkk!'

He stumbled towards the cabin, roaring flames slamming him with a wall of heat. He threw an arm across his face, quickly slapped sparks from his bushy beard, squinting and edging in. He staggered to the narrow door at the rear, where the flames hadn't reached yet.

It was nailed shut.

It stopped him in his tracks. He had thought old Trapper Jack must have been at his moonshine again and spilled some on a burning candle or something and caused the fire. But — a *door nailed-up?*

The wooden shutters over the windows on this side, not yet fully consumed by the fire, showed him other nails.

'Jesus Christ!'

He blasted with the rifle, bullets

chewing the thick, still sappy timber around bolt level — but the nails held. Looking around wildly, he lunged for the pile of logs that were yet to be chopped or sawn into firewood, grabbed a double-bladed axe and attacked the narrow door with frantic blows. He sobbed with his efforts, calling the old mountain man's name over and over.

He didn't even realize someone was shooting at him until after the third bullet blew a sliver of log from in front of his face. It carved a thin bloody line through his beard and he reared back, instinctively dropping to one knee.

Then, sprawling on his face, panting, he looked downslope and saw two riders with pack animals loaded with the stolen pelts, crossing the slope a long way down. He rolled to where he had dropped his rifle, flopped on to his belly and emptied the magazine at them, the hot, ejected brass casings hissing as they sank into the snow.

The thieves had no guts for making a stand, racing away downhill, out of range, dragging the pack animals after them. *They would keep for now.*

He threw the empty rifle from him, grabbed the axe again and battered in the door in a frenzy of wild blows.

Of course, it was too late. Old Trapper Jack had run his last wolf-line, set his last beartrap, shot his last cougar.

He was bound and gagged on his bunk . . . or what was left of it. The frame was charred and smouldering — like Trapper Jack himself.

Coughing, blinded, Cody staggered out, dragging the corpse with him. He rolled in the snow to extinguish his clothes which were burning now. The roof collapsed with an ear-shattering noise and an eruption of sparks and burning wood blasted high. Waves of heat sucked air from his lungs, singed his beard, left him dizzy and half blind.

He didn't recall rolling away from the cabin, but when his senses returned properly, he found he was halfway down the slope and the cabin was a red-glowing frame, a burned-through upright collapsing even as he stared.

He sat up, lungs raw, hacking coughs shaking him. Head hanging, chest heaving, he didn't know how much longer he sat there. Then he looked down the mountain slope — to where those two men had been when they had started shooting.

There was no sign of them now, except some scuffed snow left by their floundering horses.

'I'll find your trail, you murdering bastards!' he said aloud in a smoke-hoarse voice. 'I'll track you to Hell itself and come out the other side with your dripping scalps! There's nowhere you can hide. I'll find you if it takes the rest of my life! And when I do, that's the day you die!'

*   *   *

'*How long has he been shouting like this?*'

'*On and off for about ten minutes.*

Starts up and drifts away . . . havin' nightmares, I reckon.'

'He's delirious! That head-wound was filthy. Probably infected — and he's lost a lot of blood. He feels feverish. Have Chip haul up a bucket of well water and we'll bathe him. We must get his temperature down.'

'Curtin's dead!' They jumped as Cody shouted the words, his hands opening and closing on the rumpled sheets.

'Oh-oh, here we go again!'

'Hurry up with that well-water!'

'You're next, Willis! You get no more chance than you gave poor Trapper Jack, you son of a bitch!'

'He's sure riled about somethin'!'

'Ye-es, and I think I know what now. If I'm right, we could've made a big mistake about Catamount Cody . . . '

★　★　★

He floated up through drifting mists. 'Early morning, in the mountains.

128

Sun'll burn off the mist soon.'

'There's no mist in here. Your eyesight must be affected by the fever.'

He stiffened at the sound of the voice, turned his head sharply to the side and immediately regretted it — his brain felt loose inside his skull. He moaned and squinted but not before he glimpsed a woman seated in a chair beside the bed where he lay in a room — where?

He recognized her: Pru someone. Town councillor, had all the men buffaloed, even the judge.

Cody struggled to lift himself on to one elbow but she leaned across the bed and pushed him back gently. He stared at her, frowning, bewildered.

'What — how did I get here?'

'One of my men, young Chip Garner, found you. Heard the Singing-Stones and went to investigate. You'd apparently been thrown from your horse.' She paused and her suntanned face hardened a little. 'He back-tracked you and found another horse — with a dead man roped across it.'

After a silence he nodded — very gently. 'Recollect now. If he'd tracked back a little more, he'd have found two others dead in Kelsey's hideout.'

Her shoulders stiffened. 'You killed three men?'

'No. Just Kelsey. He killed the guard, feller called Gumbo but Gumbo nailed Dack Jameson with his last shot.'

'But you killed Kelsey?' He nodded and she asked, 'Why didn't you bring them all? There must've been spare horses.'

'Kelsey got off one last shot.' He touched his now neatly bandaged head, glanced at her sharply. 'I think you're due my thanks, ma'am.'

'I'd do the same for any wounded man.'

He managed a faint smile. 'Even a bounty hunter, huh?'

She nodded curtly, unsmiling.

'Well, I didn't bring in Gumbo or Dack, because I never killed 'em.'

Lines creased her smooth brow. 'I

don't understand your reasoning.'

'I couldn't rightfully claim the bounty on 'em, could I?' His words were curt, impatient.

Her lips parted and her gaze was steady on his pain-lined face. 'But you can claim the bounty on Arnie Kelsey — because you shot him?'

He nodded — but it was a mite too fast and he grabbed at his head, smothering a curse. 'That's right.'

'I-I've never heard of a bounty hunter with scruples before!'

'Is that what they are? Just seems right to me.'

'You raved quite a lot — about a man called Trapper Jack. It appears he was burned alive in a mountain cabin by two men — I suspect they were the ones you brought into Hopeful, to claim the bounty — Curtin and Willis?'

His mouth was a thin line now, his face as hard as she had ever seen it. *Chiselled* she thought was the best word. *Chiselled, with hard, angular lines and eyes that looked like the business end of bullets . . .*

She shivered briefly. 'Trapper Jack was your friend, I take it? Your partner in trapping for furs?'

'He was more than that — he raised me. Pulled me out of the wreck of a Conestoga wagon that had run off a cliff trying to out-distance a Lakota war party. I was all busted up — leg, arm, a wrist, concussion — I was just a shaver, mebbe four or five years old. Jack took me back to the mountains and nursed me till I was well again. Later he told me he'd lost his wife and baby son to Injuns. Never felt complete afterwards, even though he wiped out a couple dozen Sioux before he realized nothing was going to bring his family back. Guess I kinda stood in for his dead son.'

Pru frowned, and he surprised a fleeting compassion on her face, as he continued, 'Lived with Jack for years. When the war came, I walked outa the mountains and fought for the South.'

'But it sounds more like you were a

Northerner, up in Lakota country.'

'Jack found papers in the wagon. I was born in Georgia. He said it was only right I fought for the Confederates.'

'Which side did he fight on?'

'Neither — he only had one leg. One real leg, I mean — t'other was wood and leather, a contraption he made himself, whittled it out of a length of live oak, after a grizzly chewed-off the real one,' He sounded wistful. 'Tough old codger, Trapper Jack. Never even knew his second name 'til after . . . '

He stopped speaking and she waited, but he said no more. He admitted he was hungry when she asked him and she went away and returned later with a meal which he ate — or half of it. He found he wasn't anywhere near as hungry as he had thought.

She sat by the bed and rolled him a cigarette to have with his coffee. 'You were saying you learned Trapper Jack's name after — what? The cabin fire?'

She was uncomfortable at the look he gave her, but his face softened abruptly and he nodded.

'Jack Farnham — had a family in Raintree, Kentucky. A widowed sister and her daughter's brood. We had a kinda deal — that if anything happened to either of us, the other would take care of any surviving kin. In my case, I had none, but he said mebbe I'd get married sometime and if a grizz decided to see what my innards looked like, well, he'd see my share of the pelts and stuff would go to my widow — if there was one.'

'And did you get married?'

'Not me. But, like I said, Jack had a sister and her daughter's family, but there wasn't much to give 'em. We had a little ready cash for supplies and ammuntion and new traps and things but that didn't go far. The youngest girl had been born with some bone trouble and she couldn't walk. She needed a wheelchair — I made her one, which wasn't so good — it busted after a while. So when a sheriff was looking for posse men to run down a bunch of stage robbers — and was paying for it — I took the job. That was where I saw the dodger on Curtin and Willis, the *sonsabit* — the ones who killed Jack and stole our furs.'

She was looking at him strangely now. 'I think I see. You went after them, wanted the bounty to help this crippled girl.'

He flushed a little and she saw he was actually embarrassed. 'There's a doctor in Chicago, named Furse — a specialist in bone disease. Jack's sister, Lucy, wrote to him and he said if little Lurlene could go to Chicago he'd be willing to have a look at her and see if an operation — or a series of 'em, would help: there was a chance she might even be able to walk.'

'So, this is why you're in such a hurry to get what I called 'blood money'!'

He said nothing. She was breathing faster now, looking abashed and out of countenance. She twisted her hands in her lap.

'I'm afraid I always have had a big

mouth, as most folk in Hopeful will agree! Oh, Cody, I'm sorry: I've misjudged you. I don't know what else to say! How can I make it up to you?'

'I ain't worried about it — you've more than squared away for anything you figure needed it.' He gestured to the room and the bandage around his head.

'That's generous of you. I might take a little time to come to terms with it fully — '

'Don't worry about it.' His tone was clipped and it only served to make her look more embarrassed. He sighed. 'How'm I doing, anyway? When will I be able to ride into town and claim the bounty on Kelsey? Hey! How long've I been here?'

'About a day and a half. I don't think you'll be able to ride for a couple more days yet . . . '

'I don't aim to stay here that long! I mean, I'm mighty obliged for what you've done but — well, I just can't lie around here.'

'You need rest and care for a little longer.'

He saw her teeth tug at her bottom lip and she busied herself collecting the food tray and utensils, keeping her face turned from him. 'What is it? What's happened?'

Straightened, holding the tray, her back to him, she said, without turning, 'Jim Crane died early this morning.'

'Damn! Sorry to hear that.'

'There's lynch talk already. I've sent in some men to be deputized by Judge Ivers, but I don't know if Blake Ross will accept them as help. He seems to have something he wants to prove to the town — so he'll get the sheriff's job, I suppose.'

'Ross can't handle a lynch mob! He's too green — nowhere near as tough as he thinks he is. He won't be able to keep a mob from stringing up Red Higgins — not that Red don't deserve it.'

'We can't allow that to happen! With a name like Hopeful we have to help the town to live up to it! Mob rule won't do that.' A pause, and then she said, 'The judge was hoping you'd be back before anything happened, but I'm sure he didn't reckon on you being wounded like this.'

'Like what? I might've been poorly when your man brought me in but I'm OK now.'

'You're a lot weaker than you realize!'

He laughed. 'Boy, if Trapper Jack heard you say that you'd hear him laugh from here to Texas! You won't find any mountain man worth his salt who lets a bullet graze and a hatful of cuts nail him down! Hell, they'd never let me back in the mountains again.'

'Who wouldn't?' Pru was genuinely puzzled.

'The men, of course!' She still failed to understand. 'The men who live in the mountains — they're a kind of tight-knit tribe. You know — going about their business, months at a time, without seeing another living soul. We have our rendezvous, get drunk, brawl, have fun . . .'

'Is that what you call it?'

'Well, it's mostly harmless — a few busted heads or noses don't bother anyone. Let off some steam. They look out for each other. They take a liking to you, you've got friends for life, friends who'll kill for you if they have to.'

She nodded slowly. 'I think I'm beginning to understand a little. You have to measure up to their standards or else. Would they have known about your promise to Trapper Jack?'

'S'pose so. It might never've been spoken of directly, but it'd've gotten around somehow.'

'And *somehow*, those men will watch you, make sure you keep your part of the bargain?'

He nodded, serious now. 'It's their — our — unwritten code. They'll see no harm comes to me to keep me from doing what they figure I should on Jack's behalf.'

'But they won't actually help you?'

'Hell, no! It's my deal. My responsibility to see it's done. I ask for help and it'd finish me with 'em. They'd never let me anywhere near the mountains.'

'That is a very strict code! Would they — would they come and help keep down a lynch mob?'

He smiled, shaking his head slowly. 'In a town? No, ma'am! Towns and civilization are different worlds to them. Their world's up high, on the mountain-tops, close as they can get to the sky, where they can breathe easy. You got troubles down here, that's your problem — you gotta find a way to settle 'em, like they have to do theirs.'

'But that's hardly . . . tribal!'

'It's not that they don't care: it's just that fighting their own battles is the only way they know and they figure everyone else should do the same. They don't ask for help. It's the way they do things and are the stronger for it — independence, I s'pose. Responsible for their own actions. You might be surprised to know most every one of them tough bastards up there is a God-fearin' man, too.'

'And these are the people who moulded you! My God, we did badly underestimate you, Catamount Cody! I just hope it's not too late to get you on our side!'

'I'm already there, Pru. All you gotta do is fetch my clothes . . . and guns.'

9

Hang the Scum!

'You gotta get me outa here, Ross!'

Red Higgins gripped the bars of his cell door, face pressed hard against the iron, shouting down the passage.

It didn't seem to produce any result and he swore, kicked the bars, grabbed them with his good hand and shook them until they rattled in the frame.

'*Ross! You hear me? I should never've been put in here, damn you!*'

The door leading from the front office to the cell block opened and Blake Ross appeared. He stood just inside the passage for a long minute, staring at the prisoner — hearing the shouted insults and threats coming through the barred window, reaching into the cell block from the lane that ran down alongside the jail.

'You ain't gonna see no law court, Higgins!'

'We don't need judge and jury to tell us you're guilty! We *knows* it!'

'And you'll damn well pay!'

'Yeah! Hang the scum!'

'Gonna stretch your neck, Red! Shoulda been done long ago, but we'll see to it this time, you murderer!'

Higgins rattled the door again. 'Goddammit, Ross! You hear that?'

Blake Ross didn't answer but started walking slowly down to the cell where the sweating, obviously scared Higgins had jammed himself against the door — as if putting just one extra inch between himself and the gathering mob would help.

'Why don't you break up them fools?' Red demanded, gesturing to the high barred window, the growling of the gathering mob like a bunch of animals squabbling over food.

'They ain't causin' any trouble.'

'Huh! Not to you! They're threatenin' to lynch me!'

'Can't blame 'em. You should never've rid down Jim Crane.'

Red's rheumy eyes narrowed. 'He shouldn't've tried to stop me! Hell, I didn't know who it was — it was just . . . just someone in my way!'

'If you'd recognized Jim, you mean you'd've hauled rein?' Ross looked amused, smirking. 'Like hell you would!'

'Damn you, Ross! You know what I mean. I was bein' hounded — I panicked!'

'And now Jim Crane's dead, you gotta pay the piper.'

Higgins's eyes slitted. 'Mebbe I won't be the only one!'

'Well, I dunno who else would. You killed him and you're the last of the bank robbers.'

'That so?'

Just then there was a barrage of threats and the sound of a breaking bottle hurled against the stone outside wall of the cell block. Red Higgins winced, eyes widening now as he looked at the deputy.

'Well, you better do *somethin'!*' he panted.

'Man tries to stop a riled-up bunch like that and he's likely to get strung up alongside you.'

'Yeah — well, that's a possibility — an' you know that, too!'

Ross nodded slowly. 'I know what you're gonna try, Red. Give you fair warnin' — don't!'

'Or . . . ?'

'Or you could get shot while tryin' to escape.' Ross smiled crookedly as he saw the alarm on Higgins's face. 'And I wouldn't have to explain a thing . . . not one damn thing.'

Higgins's knuckles were white where they gripped the bars. 'C'mon, Ross! We done a lotta things together before you took a deputy's badge! Hell, even some after! You can't just throw me to a lynch mob!'

Ross tugged at an earlobe. 'Truth is, Red, I just dunno what else I can do. It all comes down to how well liked Jim

Crane was — an' how you ain't liked at all. 'Specially as you were caught robbin' the bank!'

'That should never've happened! If it wasn't for that damn Cody we wouldn't have this hassle.'

'*We* don't. You're the one with the hassle.'

'Aw, no! Aw, no you don't . . . '

Blake Ross stepped forward and drove a boot against Red's knuckles. The man yelped and leapt back, legs buckling and he almost fell as he clasped his bruised hand. He straightened, anger, almost, but not quite, wiping the agony from his face.

The deputy had a cocked six-gun in his hand, covering Red through the bars.

'Hey! Wait up!'

'Red, I could shoot you down and before anyone got in here to see what it was all about, I could have this door open and your body arranged so it looked like you were shot while tryin' to get past me.'

Higgins ran a tongue around dry lips:

146

he knew Ross was right — and serious.

'S'pose I yell to them fellers outside that you put me up to robbin' the bank while the whole blamed town was at Nat Palmer's funeral?'

'You'd never get past the first word, Red.'

Higgins was breathing hard now: he knew he was literally fighting for his life. 'I could try! All I gotta say is 'Ross made me rob the bank!' Half a dozen words! I'd get them out, you know I would.'

Ross shook his head slowly. 'Every time you open your mouth, you dig your grave deeper, you damn fool!'

Red knew that was true but he was desperate now, actually looked towards the barred window as the men outside hurled more threats.

'Come an' get me, you loud-mouthed bastards! You're all talk! You even got Ross too scared to try 'n stop you! He's got a gun on me and the door's still locked! I can't escape!' Red smiled at Ross, almost challengingly. 'Can I, Deputy?'

'By hell, you take some chances, Red!'

The deputy didn't know what to do. He had hesitated too long. Red had said his piece and set the scene!

He could shoot him now, through the bars — but the cell-door keys were still hanging in the front office. He would not have time to get them, open the door, and arrange things so it looked as if Red had somehow managed to get the door open and tried to get past Ross. And if he left him alone while he went to fetch the keys, the man would yell his head off, saying way too much!

The son of a bitch had turned the tables on him.

Then, just to make it perfect —

'Come on, you men. Break this up! Take that whiskey back into the saloon where it belongs and drink it there. You can be brave as you like in the bar, but I'll shoot the first one makes a move to drag Red Higgins out and tries to lynch him.'

It was Catamount Cody's voice.

148

Cody was backed by three of the six Block R crew Pru Riordan had sent into town earlier for deputization by Judge Ivers. These three were the only ones still part-way sober. The others were still in the saloon.

Pru had ridden in with Cody — he had ignored her pleas not to leave his bed so soon — along with young Chip Garner who was eager to be in on this drama.

Not that the kid wanted to help lynch Red Higgins, or anyone else for that matter, but he figured if he showed up and backed Cody as well as his limited experience allowed, it would raise his standing with the rough Block R crew and they would ease up on their joshing and teasing.

Pru had not been keen, but Cody had watched, somewhat amused, as the kid sweet-talked her around. He saw she favoured him, like a kid brother, and when she noticed Cody watching, her cheeks coloured. She had looked pretty defiant when she had finally given in.

'All right, Chip, all right! You've worn me down.' Her eyes flashed at Cody as he smiled slightly. 'Cody, I make you responsible for Chip's safety. You have any objections to that?'

'None. I feel obligated, anyway, seeing as he brought me in from the Singing-Stones.'

Chip looked uncomfortable. 'Aw — it was the only thing to do. I couldn't leave you out there.'

'No, you couldn't, but some men might've. You stay behind me and the others, kid, till we see just how dangerous this lynch mob is.'

It was disappointing to find that half of the men Pru had sent in to help Ross were drinking their time away in the bar of the Starlight saloon.

Pru was so angry, she could barely speak, fired the three drunks on the spot. Two didn't care, but the third, a rugged man named Perry, started to cuss her out. Cody picked up a bung-starter from the bar top and slammed the man across the head. He folded, one arm hooked through the brass footrail, bleeding head resting on the damp sawdust.

The saloon regulars watched, glad of the entertainment. Cody hefted the bung-starter on its long, lawyer-cane handle, challenging the other two — no takers. They finished their drinks, picked up their unconscious companion and headed for the rear door.

Pru glared at Barney Starr, the saloon owner, his completely bald head gleaming with sweat.

'Damn you, Barney! I'll see you don't get any more custom from Block R.' She looked coldly around the room, frowned slightly. 'Is someone footing the bill for all this booze that's flowing here? Or are you giving drinks on the house?'

Starr shrugged. 'Mebbe I was feelin' generous.'

That brought scattered laughter and a cheer from the drinkers, several raising their glasses in a toast to Starr.

'Or maybe you just wanted to get folk in the right mood for a lynch party,' Cody told him.

He was a big man, Barney Starr, and he had eyes that had seen it all over the years from his side of the bar. But when his gaze locked with Cody's he straightened his face.

'Mister, I run my saloon the way I want. I don't tell you how to run your business.' Slyly, he smiled crookedly, and winked at the expectant crowd. 'Not that I know anythin' about bounty-huntin'.'

'Well, ain't much to know, really. You just track your man down and if you're lucky enough to square-off with him you just draw your gun — like this — and either put a bullet in him, or slam him over the head — *like this!*'

Cody took one long stride closer to the bar, reached across the counter, and the side of his heavy Colt slammed Barney on the naked temple. Before dropping out of sight behind the bar,

Starr's groping arm knocked a whole row of bottles and glasses from the counter. The drinkers jumped back, watching Cody warily as he raked a cold gaze around the room.

'I'm getting a sawn-off Greener and then I'm going down to the jailhouse to sit in front of Red Higgins's cell. I don't want to see any of your ugly faces coming towards me down the passage — savvy?'

'Hey! You ain't the sheriff yet!' someone called.

'Don't have to be. The Greener's all the authority I need to stop a lynching.'

'Hell! Jim Crane was a damn decent man! I heard he give you a shirt and a new pair of boots!'

'He did, and I'm mighty grateful. As you say, Jim was a decent man — hard to come by someone as decent most times. But you think he'd want to see a lynch party in his town? Specially when Red's headed for the gallows anyway . . . You want to show Jim Crane the respect you say you had for him, think

153

about that — then have one more drink for the trail and head on home.' He smiled thinly. 'You might even wake up in the morning without a hangover.'

'I ain't gonna be pushed around by no bounty-hunter!' Whoever said it stayed hidden in the middle of the crowd, and several others murmured what might have been support.

'You didn't mind him being a bounty-hunter when he stopped Red and his men from stealing your savings!' Pru Riordan snapped, eyes flashing.

'An' *you* din' want him to be offered the sheriff's job because he *was* a bounty hunter!'

That one got a small, ragged cheer and Pru squared up to the jeering men.

'I know. But I got it wrong . . . Oh, yes, you may look surprised that I'd admit to it, but it's true. Here and now's not the place to go into details, but if Jim Crane was a decent man, then so is Catamount Cody. Take my word for it!'

There was silence — astonished silence. For Pru Riordan was not someone noted for admitting a mistake under any circumstances.

It did more to break up the embryo lynch party than Cody's presence or his cocked pistol . . .

* * *

They moved on down to the jailhouse, saw the ragged line of hard-drinkers crowding into the alley beside the jail, and Cody moved right in — with young Chip Garner at his side, the kid's face pale but determined as he licked his lips and tightened his grip on the Winchester carbine he held. The other three Block R men stood by, guns in hands.

It took only one shot from Cody's Colt to back up his words as he told the men to take themselves back to the saloon or their homes.

'Start moving, fellers.' He gestured with the smoking Colt barrel. 'That one was into the air. I start aiming lower

from now on — round about foot level
. . . What'll it be?'

Growling, antagonistic, but well aware
of Cody's prowess with firearms, the
mob broke up, shuffling out of the lane.

An angry Blake Ross was standing on
the front landing of the law office when
Cody and Chip came out behind the
dispersing men. Pru Riordan was
settling into the saddle of her palomino
stallion near the hitch rail.

The deputy held a rifle and he
pointed it at Cody.

'Just what the hell you think you're
doin'?'

'What you should've done: broke up
that lynch mob.'

'I'll do things in my own good time
— and my way. I don't need no help
from no bounty-hunter!'

'Seems I've heard that before, Ross,
but why look a gift horse in the mouth?'

'You just stay outa things that don't
concern you! I'm the one wearin' the
badge here.'

'And that deputy's star comes with

certain responsibilities, Blake,' Pru said suddenly, drawing the deputy's attention. 'Not allowing a bunch of drunks to take the law into their own hands is one of them — and high priority, at that. You seem to have been more than a little slow.'

'I was workin' towards it! I had my own problems with Red to settle first!'

'How is he?' Cody asked quietly. 'Still cringing in his cell? I mean, he hasn't tried to escape — no, guess he wouldn't want to risk getting shot doing that.'

Ross was glad to get out from under Pru's stare and he swung back towards Cody. 'What the hell does that mean?'

Cody raised his eyebrows. 'Sounded plain enough to me — my best American.'

'You hintin' that I'd want to shoot Red?'

'Now that's a queer thing to say.'

Blake Ross started to bristle, then seemed to realize Cody was baiting him and made an obvious effort to stay calm.

'Well, you're the queer one. I dunno what the hell you're tryin' to say, but I'm tellin' you the safest place for Red Higgins is right where he is now — in my cell block!'

'And so it should be, Ross. You won't mind if I sit in for a spell, kinda relieve you so you can do other duties?'

'Listen, I don't need you — either to tell me my duties or to sit in. You got no authority here, Cody. Time you realized that.'

'Not quite true, Blake,' Pru said, watching the deputy's head snap around. 'Judge Ivers has deputized Cody: he has every right to help guard the prisoner . . . and to have a say in breaking up any mob that tries to form.'

Ross did not like that. For a wild moment, Pru felt her heart skip a beat as Ross looked at Cody with outright murder in his eyes. But the deputy got himself under control.

'Then — you got no authority over me, Cody! You're just another deputy, an' seein' as I've been in the job longer, guess that makes me senior man.'

'Makes you something, Ross. But I'm answerable only to the judge. He's given me a free hand to keep this town under control. With or without you.'

Ross frowned at Pru. 'That gospel?'

'Yes, Blake, it is.'

'Well, *dammittohell!* By Godfrey, I got a good mind to turn in my badge and to hell with this lousy town and everyone in it!' When they said nothing, he added bitterly, 'Don't damn well show much confidence in me, does it?'

'Be honest with yourself, Blake,' Pru said, uncharacteristically temperate, 'Cody is better with a gun than you . . . ' She was about to add *and a lot of other things, too*, but refrained. 'He's dealt with killers and murderous drunks for years. The judge just figured it was a wise move to have a man of Cody's experience to back you up.'

'Back me *up* . . . ?' Ross's thundercloud face straightened a little. He nodded. 'Yeah, well, that's OK. Long as he realizes he ain't in charge.'

Cody shook his head slowly but remained silent.

He actually felt a little sorry for Ross: the man had bullied and bluffed his way through his job for a long time and now, just when he figured he would be able to step into the dead sheriff's shoes, along comes a bounty hunter, handy with guns and fists — *handier* with guns and fists than Ross himself — and forces him to look candidly at himself and — *perhaps* — admit that he wasn't the hot-shot he tried to convince folk he was.

But Cody had a niggling twinge deep down, warning him that maybe, just maybe, there was another reason for Ross's hostility and reluctance to have Cody's help.

And it had more than a little to do with Red Higgins.

10

Chip

Chip Garner was feeling pretty damn good.

Here he was, doing something with a heap of responsibility and *trusted* to do it properly! No constant supervision or hassling as it was back on the ranch while he struggled to master the chores an unsympathetic — maybe jealous — ranch crew threw his way.

It was mighty hard when a man — or a kid! — was seen to be the boss's favourite. It generated a lot of hostility and the only way these cowhands could see to rid themselves of it — without losing their jobs — was to take out their frustrations by riding him hard: under the guise of 'teaching him the ropes'.

He had a good share of inner fortitude — *guts* — that surprised him at times and enabled him to not only shrug off being pushed around, but to make a tolerable effort at carrying out the harsh orders.

There had been a few times when Pru, noting some harassment, or implication of it, had tried to intervene. But he had felt quite proud of himself when each time he had refused to admit to the misery that had been forced upon him, and even depreciated himself by claiming aloud he was so green he was making the chores much harder than they needed to be.

Pru was not fool enough to swallow this, but admired him silently for trying to tough it out.

'Well, don't be afraid to ask how things are done, Chip.' She raked a cool gaze around at the nearby crew who were pretending to go about their chores, though they had their ears hanging out a mile. 'It's the best, perhaps the only, way to learn. Benefit from others' experience: isn't that so, men? You all had to learn these things when you first started, didn't you?'

There were murmurs of grudging agreement and Pru smiled and returned to her big ranch house.

It didn't really help Chip Garner, her brief checks on his 'progress'. All it did was hone the edge of the crew's hostility: at least he had managed to get it across that it was better if she didn't invite him up to the house. Oh, he knew she had his welfare at heart, teaching him to read and write better, but after each session he had to return to the bunkhouse — and find a snake in his bed, or his boots filled with molasses and, once, his bunk collapsed because the screws holding it together had been removed in his absence.

Chip, although he didn't realize it, was growing tougher.

He even protested sometimes now when the worst of the crew thought up some demeaning chore that he knew damn well was not even necessary only as an instrument to humiliate him.

'I don't have time,' he told Larsen,

one of the top-hands who seemed to delight in making Chip's life as hard as possible, when he had been delegated to clean out the tick trough the cattle were driven through regularly. The milky solution left a deposit when it settled and sometimes this grew thick enough to block the drain plugs.

It was a filthy chore, cleaning it: a man had to wade through the sludge, half-choked by the pungent odours of the sediment. He was likely to stink of it for days and Larsen knew Pru was expecting Chip to escort her to church tomorrow.

'You don't have time!' Larsen said, blinking in surprise at the kid's temerity. 'Hey, you fellers hear that? The kid's pushed for *time!*'

'Well, I was you, Swede, I'd teach him a lesson about 'time' and what it means on Block R.'

The men grinned at the wrangler's sly advice.

Larsen showed his decayed teeth, hands on his big hips as he leaned towards the kid, whose face was as pale as one of the clouds scudding across the blue sky.

'Wrangler's right, kid, you need a lesson. Tell you what I'm gonna do — you take the pack horses down to the creek and water 'em. You know, pack horses? Not for ridin', so you walk, an' lead 'em. You take three or four at a time, let 'em frolic and drink, bring 'em back, then take another bunch. Get it?'

Chip looked anxiously at the big corral of milling pack animals. There were at least twenty! He glanced to the west. 'It'll be dark before I finish!'

'Well, if you're slow, I guess it will be.'

'By the time I get cleaned up, Cookie will have stopped servin' supper.'

'Aw, shucks, so he will — he's one for stickin' to his own timetable. But that don't matter.' Larsen leaned closer, his breath sour. ''Cause after you water the pack hosses, then you clean out the tick trough. Easy to do. Just hang a few lanterns along the back wall of the barn an' you'll see OK. No sun to stir up them fumes.'

'I see OK right now, Swede!' the kid said, almost breathless but knowing he had to stand up for himself here or conditions would never improve. 'I'll water the pack horses — then I'll see if Cookie's got a little supper left over. *Then* I'll turn in and after I come back from escortin' Pru to church in the mornin', *then* I'll clean the tick trough — if you'll show me how.'

Larsen's big eyes widened and the men listening were stunned at first, then began to laugh.

'You know Pru said I was to learn from experience,' Chip went on. 'I'll just ask her on the way to church if she feels the trough needs cleanin' before we push the south pastures' herd through it next week, and if you'd be the one to show me what to do. I guess she'll figure you've got enough experience to teach me all I need to know.'

'Hey, Swede! He's got you!' the wrangler said, almost unable to get out the words, he was laughing so much. 'You know what Pru said — 'You men set the boy an example, *show him what's to be done, and I'll dock the pay, or worse, if this harassment of him keeps up and anyone is foolish enough to refuse to show him what he needs to know'.*'

Swede Larsen glanced towards the house, saw Pru hanging out some washing and glared at Chip Garner.

'There'll be another time, kid! And you can take it as gospel that I'll be just waitin' for it!'

Chip knew he would pay for this but, even though his heart hammered wildly and his stomach was tight and knotted as a greehorn's lariat, he still felt proud. *This was a start, and it had been a long time coming — perhaps, too long.*

But, as it worked out, he didn't have to worry about Swede's threat after going to town. When Pru found her crew in the saloon instead of helping to see a lynch mob didn't drag Red Higgins out of the jail, Swede Larsen was one of the men she fired for failing to follow her orders.

Chip had been there and watched soberly as Larsen and another man called Cimarron carried out Perry who had had his head busted by Cody. As they manoeuvred the unconscious man through the narrow rear door, Larsen's gaze had found Chip amongst the watching audience. His stare was murderous and caused Chip's belly to do somersaults, but Pru solved his worries by placing him in the jailhouse as back up to Blake Ross: he was unlikely to run across Swede there.

He had wished he would be sharing the guard duty with Cody, but the fact that Pru was willing to leave him be without checking every few minutes gave his ego and esteem a boost.

The town had quietened down by about eleven o'clock that night, a few drunks wandering the streets. Blake Ross grew restless: he saw it as mandatory that he kept the town streets clear of drunks and felt this night it was even more important to do so.

'Kid, you be all right here for about half an hour?'

Chip Garner blinked as he heated coffee over the small stove in the law office.

'You mean alone?'

'You won't be alone. Red's here, or in his cell — and don't you forget it! You check regular on that son of a bitch, OK?' Ross reached down his hat, jammed it on, pulled out his Colt and checked the loads. Then he took a carbine from the rack and started for the street door.

'I'm just gonna clear the streets. Don't go to sleep.'

'No, sir!' Chip said, mildly outraged at the suggestion. 'You don't have to worry none about Red Higgins — I'll guard him properly and he'll be here when you get back.'

'He damn well better be,' Ross said, and, as he went out into the night, added, 'Don't open that cell door for *anythin'*, savvy? Not — for — anythin'!'

'I'm not stupid!' Chip snapped as Ross left.

Chip made coffee and sipped it, scalding his mouth. Grimacing, he set the mug down on the desk, decided to let it stand and cool a little. He heard Red Higgins coughing, opened the cell block door and looked along the passage to Red's cell.

'You all right, Red?'

'Stupid question! How the hell would I be 'all right'? Hey — I smell coffee?'

'Just brewed some, lettin' it cool.'

'How about a cup? I ain't gonna get much damn sleep tonight.'

Chip hesitated. Ross had told Red when he served his supper hours ago that it was the last grub and drink he'd have before sun up. Maybe the last — ever.

'If you live long enough to see another sun up!' Ross had added cruelly.

Maybe Ross was right. Even though the town seemed to have cooled off since Cody had stepped in, it was still possible this might be Red's last night in this world.

170

'Yeah — OK, I'll bring you a cup.'

'How about a cracker, too?'

'Don't push it, Red!'

Higgins laughed. 'Hey, you sounded almost tough then, kid! You learnin' to speak up for yourself, huh?'

Chip felt himself flushing even though he was out of sight of Red's cell as he poured a mug of coffee. But then he smiled thinly.

Yeah! He was learning to speak up for himself! How about that!

He hesitated, then shrugged and reached into the pottery jar and took out two crumbling crackers. Carrying these in his left hand and the coffee mug in his right, he made his way down to Red's cell.

There wasn't much light in here, just two lamps on the passage wall, no light in the cell itself, making for a lot of shadows.

Which is why Chip didn't see Red Higgins right away.

Then he did and sucked in a sharp breath, swearing mildly as some hot coffee spilled on to his wrist.

Higgins was sprawled on the floor by his bunk, face down, legs catching some light from the passage, his upper body in shadow.

There was a long smear of blood beside him on the stone floor coming from beneath him.

Chip's first instinct was to go fetch the keys and open the door so he could examine Red. But common sense prevailed — and swiftly — knowing that was the last thing he should do.

Leaning against the bars, trying to get a better look at Red, he said; 'What're you doin', Red? Oh, I can see you're lyin' on the floor, hopin' I'll open up and come in, but I ain't doin' that. So, whatever you're plannin' won't work!'

Red made no move or answer.

'C'mon, Red! Quit foolin' around. I ain't fallin' for any of your tricks!' Still no sign of life from the prisoner and Chip frowned: *he didn't like all that blood! Where did it come from . . . ?* 'I'm taking the coffee and crackers back

to the front office, Red, and I ain't comin'
down here again until Blake gets back.'

He had taken five steps down the
passage when he heard Red groan, then
say in a gasping voice, 'Kid, I need the
doc! Shoulder wound's busted open.
Bleedin' like a stuck hog!'

Chip stopped, turned to face back
towards the cell door, frowning. 'How'd
that happen?'

'Fell — staggered into bunk post
— corner caught the wound. Jesus, kid!
I-I ain't tryin' anythin'! Too damn
woozy . . . for that. Just go fetch the
. . . sawbones, please!'

Chip went closer to the cell, saw that
Red had struggled to a sitting position
now, propped halfway erect against the
bunk upright. His eyelids were drooping, mouth slack. His left shirt sleeve
was soaked with blood and more ran
down to his limp hand where it rested
on the floor.

'I-I'm bleedin' to death, kid. They
won't have to worry none about
hangin' me . . . '

'I–I'll see if I can get Doc Timmins down here. Red, you stay right there!'

As Chip turned away and hurried down the passage he realized what a stupid remark that last one was. He went into the office, set down coffee and crackers on the desk and reached for his hat.

He jumped when the street door opened and Blake Ross strode in. The deputy stopped as he made to remove his hat when he saw Chip's face.

'The hell's wrong?'

'It's Red!' Chip sounded mighty relieved now that Ross was back: any decision was no longer his. 'His arm wound's bleedin' somethin' awful. I was just goin' to get Doc Timmins.'

'You wait up! Red's tryin' somethin' on.'

Ross was already opening the door to the cell block.

'No, Blake, there's blood everywhere.'

Chip Garner hurried after the deputy and Ross was standing at the cell door, staring in when Chip caught up.

'Grab one of them wall lanterns.'

Chip took one off its stand and Ross snatched it, held it high, letting the light wash over Red Higgins. The man was still propped against the bunk post, slack, face haggard, sitting in a pool of blood now. Lustreless eyes sought Ross.

'I'm dyin' . . . '

'You're pullin' somethin', that's what you're doin', Red!'

'Aw, look at all that blood, Blake!'

'Yeah, yeah, I see it.' Ross's teeth tugged at his lower lip. 'Seems a lot . . . All right, go fetch the damn sawbones. I'll stay right here an' keep an eye on this tricky son of a bitch.'

Chip ran down the passage and out through the law office into the night time Main Street of Hopeful. It was almost deserted now: a couple of cowboys sitting on the porch steps outside the saloon, quietly sharing a bottle of whiskey; Dan Cannon, the night-watchman at Horan's Ice Works taking a leak against the wall near the side door just around the corner from Main; Will Bates, the night clerk at the stage depot, yawning as he leaned in the doorway, smoking his pipe, waiting for the late stage from Federation, and a couple of pariah dogs sniffing the trash that had collected in the gutters.

As Chip jog-trotted past the saloon one of the drinkers called, 'Come an' have a snort, kid, put hair on your chest.'

Chip flushed, slowing involuntarily: it was Swede Larsen's voice and his companion laughing with him was Dusty, the other man who had been fired by Pru.

'No, thanks, Swede, I'm on an errand.'

'Don't get lost, you dummy!' Swede called, the words slurred.

Chip ran on and hammered on the door of the infirmary where the usual nightlight burned. His knock was answered after the third time and the sleepy nurse stared out at him, pushing strands of hair back from her face. She stifled a yawn.

'We need Doc quick, down at the jail,' Chip panted.

She squinted at him, blinking, trying to wake up fully, a middle-aged woman. 'Doc's not here. There's been a brush fire and someone badly burned out at the logging camp. Reckon he won't be back till mornin'.'

'Oh! We-we got a prisoner bleedin' like a pig with it's throat cut. Can you come?'

She glanced back over her shoulder even as she shook her head. 'Can't. I'm alone here and got three patients to look after. Put a pad over the wound an' bind it tightly. If it don't stop, try a tourniquet — '

'Wh-what the hell's that?'

'Watch your language, young man! It's a strap, or even a rolled neckerchief, tied tightly over the artery leadin' to the wound. Where's it bleeding?'

Chip told her and she said it would be easy to apply a tourniquet around the arm, just above the elbow.

'Just remember to slack it off every

fifteen minutes so there's no chance of gangrene.'

He went away, muttering the directions to himself.

'Hey! What's your hurry, kid?'

Chip stopped, snapping his head up, saw Swede and Dusty lumbering towards him. He gasped, hesitated, then started to sprint away.

'Hey, you yallerbelly!' Swede shouted, waving the almost empty bottle of whiskey now. 'Come back here! Go get him, Dust — '

Dusty's feet tangled and he sprawled. Swede, feeling the effects of his booze, cussed loudly and staggered after Chip. The kid easily out-distanced him and Larsen soon gave up, shouting, 'Hell wi' you, kid. I-I'll see you before I quit this lousy town . . . '

'Sshh!' Dusty said, putting a dirty finger across his lips. 'You'll bring Ross back, an' he said he'll toss us in the cells we don't stay quiet.'

'Hell wi' Ross, too!' Larsen shouted recklessly and someone lifted a window above the hotel balcony and called,

'Be quiet, you drunken fools, or I'll fetch the deputy!'

Another window scraped up and a second voice called more or less the same thing — maybe they didn't realize they were making as much, if not more, noise than the drunks.

Swede made a snarling and insulting dismissal and put his arm about Dusty's shoulders. They staggered down the nearest alley, singing out of tune, deliberately loud.

Out of breath, relieved to find he hadn't been pursued, Chip closed the office door quietly behind him, gulped a few breaths and went into the cellblock.

He stopped dead in his tracks as he heard Red Higgins saying angrily, 'Well, I'm tellin' you for the last time, Ross, you get me outa here, and I mean now, or I'm gonna tell anyone who'll listen was you organized for me and the boys to rob the bank!'

'You think anyone'd believe you?'

Deputy Ross snapped sourly.

'Why not? You been bitchin' they don't pay you enough — everyone knows that. Like they know you were after Nate Palmer's job. An' only you an' Palmer were s'posed to know that money'd be in the bank ready for shippin' to Federation. Folk ain't as dumb as you think. They'll soon figure out I'm talkin' gospel.'

'You won't be talkin' at all, you damn fool!'

'What you gonna do? Shoot me in my cell? Won't look too good, with my wound all bloody and Doc Timmins due back any minute, so you better think of somethin' pronto. Aw, shit!'

Higgins stared through the bars past Ross's shoulder as Chip moved at the end of the passage: it was obvious from the look on the kid's sweating face that he had heard everything.

'Stop him!' Red yelled, as Ross spun around, hand instinctively reaching for his Colt. 'He must've heard!'

Ross's gun came up as Chip lunged

for the door and he triggered twice. His lead knocked the kid hard against the wall and he bounced off, hit the door and fell sprawling.

'Jesus!' Red breathed. 'You stopped him all right! Dead in his tracks!'

Ross's face was tight, eyes slitted, as he rounded on the prisoner. Red's hand was bloody where it held the bars and suddenly the man stepped back as he saw Ross's face change.

'No! Wait up! I — '

' 'Bout time I stopped you, too, Red!'

11

Dead Man Talks

Pru had been awakened by the shouting — sounded like a couple of guests here in the hotel were arguing with some drunks down in the street. There were distant, running footsteps, too. *Surely not the lynch mob reforming!*

She was tired and irritable from being woken up, threw back the counterpane and went to the window. Down in the badly lit street, she saw Swede Larsen and Dusty, drunk and staggering towards an alley, yelling insults at two people hanging out of hotel windows just along from her room.

'You're making as much noise as those drunks!' she called irritably. 'Go back to sleep so we can all do the same!'

She slammed down her window and stood there a few moments. Darn it! She was fully awake now. She stiffened. She had just realized that that other dark form she had glimpsed running down the street towards the law office was Chip Garner.

'What on earth has happened now?' she asked herself exasperatedly, already reaching for her shirt and trousers draped over the bedside chair.

She couldn't possibly try to go back to sleep now.

Hesitating, she raised the window again and looked out. No sign of her drunken cowhands or Chip Garner now: the night street was deserted, shadows slashed here and there by blades of drab moonlight.

We-ell, maybe it was nothing after all. She was debating it and decided that, as she was dressed, she might as well go down to the jailhouse, take Chip a cup of coffee, perhaps spend a half-hour talking with him, help pass the dreary time of nightwatch.

He was a good kid, *so like Will, her young brother who had drowned in Maiburn Creek all those years ago . . .*

She stopped that particular thought with a wrenching effort, knotting up inside as always.

Maybe one day she would come to terms with the knowledge that had she taken time to show Will, when crossing a river with his horse, how to slip out of the saddle and hang on to his mount's mane, allowing the horse to do the swimming — as her father had requested her to do — then he might still be alive. And almost exactly Chip's age — and temperament. *So alike, in so many ways . . .*

She stiffened. Just as she was closing the window again, there was a sound like someone hammering nails — irregular tapping, but very reminiscent of that sound.

But at this time of night?

Almost at once she recognized the sound for what it really was: muffled gunfire, coming from the jailhouse . . .

Red Higgins lay dead and bleeding just inside the entrance to his cell. He was on his back, sightless eyes staring up at the stained ceiling.

Chip Garner was lying on his face near the office doorway at the other end of the passage, blood seeping out from beneath his body.

About midway between the two stood Blake Ross, reloading his smoking Colt, hands shaking a little — not much, but enough for him to know he had made his commitment now and if he wanted to pull off this deal properly, he had to get moving.

But he didn't aim to do that with a half-empty pistol in his holster. He snapped the loading gate closed, turned the cylinder a couple of times to make sure it was revolving smoothly, and leathered the gun. He looked from the cell to the sprawled body just inside the office door and then moved swiftly and unlocked the barred door. He went in and knelt beside Red Higgins, feeling for a neck pulse. Ross smiled thinly: nary a sign. At least Red couldn't implicate him in the killing of Chip Garner, or the unsuccessful bank robbery, sure not in any of the other small but lucrative deals they had worked together over the last few months, ever since he had learned for sure Nate Palmer had no intention of recommending him for the sheriff's position when and if he ever retired — *or maybe was killed in the line of duty!*

That had given Ross some food for thought and he had swallowed a lot of whiskey before Fate threw the solution in his lap.

He had been taking one of his rides around the county that Palmer had turned into a monthly chore, picking up information about riders seen in the area, any complaints about rustling, fences, water rights, or other range disputes: this was why Nate Palmer ran such a good county and town — he kept his finger on the pulse of things, nipped a lot of trouble in the bud before it got out of hand.

Bonnie Steele had complained three of her prime steers had been rustled a couple of nights back and her men had tracked the thieves into the Banjo Canyon country but lost them somewhere in that tangle.

Likely scared to go after 'em in that maze! Ross thought silently. But Ross was a good tracker, so had landed the chore of finding the rustlers.

But he didn't fancy riding into that tangle of canyons after wideloopers — most would try to shoot their way out of trouble if cornered, knowing a rope was all they could expect as an alternative.

But he decided to cut through part of the canyons on his way back so he could put it in his report: *No tracks found*. It would satisfy Palmer, for a while . . . he hoped.

Unfortunately, although it was true he did not find any tracks, he ran smack into Arnie Kelsey and Dack Armstrong working a running-iron beside a waterhole where Ross had figured to slake his own and his mount's thirsts.

They were edgy and Dack had a rifle on Ross before he knew it.

'Hell, it's that go-for-'em deputy, Arnie. See how tough he is now, away from Palmer backin' him, eh?'

'Ah, I don't feel like talkin',' Arnie had growled, his mouth swollen from where a flying hoof from one of Bonnie Steele's stolen steers had caught him squarely. 'Shoot the son of a bitch and be done with it. We'll bury him in here. Never be found.'

'Hold up! Hold up!' Blake Ross said swiftly, as Dack lifted his rifle barrel. 'Wait! Listen, I know where you can make a hundred times what these beeves'll fetch — gospel!'

'Yeah?' Arnie showed mild interest and Dack swore softly: he was just about to nail this arrogant deputy. 'You don't make anywheres near that much, Deputy.'

Dack laughed at Ross's face and the way his hands came up in front of his eyes as if he was getting ready to catch bullets. 'You got him there, Arne!'

Ross licked his lips. 'I tell you it's gospel — on the Federation stage, a strongbox holdin' the mines' payroll.'

'Hell, you think we're dumb? That payroll don't get sent till the end of the month and it goes with half a dozen outriders.'

Blake was shaking his head before Kelsey finished. 'Not this time. Federal Minerals is sellin' out to Consolidated Mines in Denver. Consolidated's bringin' in their own crew so Federal has to pay off the crew workin' for 'em now. Palmer's gettin' married so they're payin' him plenty to ride along as a sort of weddin' present and for him to act as undercover guard. He needs the extra money.'

Arnie and Dack exchanged glances: *could this be true? A golden chance at one big job that would set them up so they could head back to Kelsey's native*

Canada . . . .He had too many Wanted dodgers on him out here and he knew it was only a matter of time before the Federal Marshals were on his trail.

'Maybe you better tell us some more,' Kelsey said, dry-mouthed, and Dack nodded his agreement.

'I got details of route and timetables.' Blake stopped, let that sink in, then said slowly, 'Got 'em without Nate knowin'. Just one thing you gotta do, though . . . '

Kelsey drew his gun and cocked it. 'And what might that be . . . ? You try to get smart with us, Ross, and you're dead in your tracks!'

Ross held up a hand quickly. 'Not tryin' to pull nothin'. Just want you to . . . ' He hesitated, breathing fast now: almost afraid to say his next words. Again Ross's hands came up as if they could protect him from gunfire. 'You gotta swear you'll kill Nate Palmer!'

The silence in the camp was heavy: even the newly branded cows had stopped their complaints. The rustlers exchanged glances: now that could be a *good* idea!

'You want to split this three ways?' Dack asked.

Ross shook his head. 'No. You nail Palmer and I'll settle for a quarter share.'

'Or whatever we decide to let you have.'

Ross made himself straighten and clamped his jaw hard as he set his gaze on Kelsey. 'Play it fair, Arnie. It's the best for everyone in the long run.'

'You really believe that?' Dack asked, grinning tightly.

'I decide what's best,' cut in Kelsey. 'Why you want Nate dead? Not that I don't think it would suit him: make a fine-lookin' corpse, old Nate would — the son of a bitch! I gotta score of my own to settle with that bastard!'

Dack guffawed and Ross told them how he wanted the sheriff's position — badly. 'I can make Hopeful mine! I got advance information on what's gonna happen to the town — railroad spur's comin': they've already started buyin' up land; they're gonna dam Federation Creek and pipe water to Cartwheel Meadows — make it a giant salad bowl. Cattle pens are gonna be built, and that means hotels, saloons and cathouses for the trail men — whole heap of stuff, Arnie. You boys come in with me on this and we'll all be rich.'

Of course, Kelsey and Armstrong were all for it now. Ross knew they would double-cross him at the first chance, but as long as they killed Palmer it would suit him: Nate was so popular there would be one helluva hue-and-cry and it was doubtful Kelsey and Dack would live long once the posses started scouring the country for them.

But . . .

Cody had chanced along and eventually settled Arnie and Dack's careers for them. That suited Ross fine — except it made the town want Cody for the new sheriff even more. *And the sonuva had* turned up in time to stop the bank robbery! Talk about luck — good and bad: good for Cody, pretty damn bad for Ross and his plans.

He had plenty to settle with Cata-mount Cody.

But, for now, he had to get moving and arrange things in the cell block. The shots may not have been heard, seeing as they were fired within the jail's stone walls, but it had to look right for whoever showed up to find both Red and the kid lying dead and bloody . . .

He was still stooping over young Chip when he heard the street door open. He swore: goddammit, the kid must've left it unlocked when he'd gone to fetch the doctor and hadn't stopped to lock it after he'd come back.

Pru's enquiring voice reached him faintly through the heavy wooden door leading to the office and, cursing, he rose from his crouched position as she entered the passage.

'I heard shooting and — my God!

What's happened?' She knelt swiftly beside Chip. 'Oh, no!'

'Red killed him,' Blake Ross told her, taking her by the shoulders and lifting her to her feet.

She wrenched her horrified eyes from Chip and stared up into Ross's face. 'How on earth did — ?'

'Kid was careless — too trustin'. Red must've tore open that shoulder wound and made it bleed, drippin' his blood all round the cell to make it look worse. Kid was convinced he was haemorraghin', must've opened the cell and went to look for hisself. He ran past me, yellin', all excited, sayin' he'd go fetch Doc Timmins, but he must've forgot to lock Red in. I went to get some rags, Red lyin' on the floor unconscious, as I thought. I was takin' 'em down to the cell just as the kid come burstin' in and said Doc was outa town. I dunno where he got it, but Red had a gun — mebbe lifted it from Chip without the kid knowin' when he was in the cell: Red was good at that kinda thing. Anyway he had the damn gun, however he got hold of it!' Ross paused briefly, trying to look contrite. 'Chip yelled a warnin' to me and Red fired. Bullet hit Chip and by then I had my gun out and I nailed Red, but it was too late for Chip.'

Pru frowned, thinking about this. 'Chip would know if his gun had been taken from his holster, surely?'

'Well, you'd think so. I mean, he was foolish even goin' into Red's cell, but to wear his gun in as well . . . ' He shook his head slowly. 'I guess he thought he was helpin' me, but he was still pretty much a greenhorn.'

'N-no, he's lyin', Pru!'

Blake Ross felt his scalp prickle at the gasping sound of Chip Garner's voice, coming from the floor. The kid lay there, coughing blood now, one hand being held by Pru as she hastily dropped to a knee beside him, smoothing his sweaty brow with a slim hand. Life was fluttering, barely hovering in Chip's pale-blue eyes.

'Ross shot me, Pru. Then Red. He set

up the bank robbery. Red was gonna tell to save his own neck from . . . the . . . mob . . . '

Pru, pale now, lunged to her feet, tears blurring her vision. Blake grabbed her quickly, pinning her arms. 'Damn you, kid!' he snarled down at the wounded Chip.

He lifted his Colt and Pru fought and kicked and got an arm free, raking at Ross's eyes. He felt the sting as nails tore at his flesh and flung her against the stone wall with an angry grunt. She gasped as she struck the wall hard and slumped to a sitting position on the floor, stunned.

Ross was quivering, gun pointed at Pru, undecided what to do. Dare he shoot someone as important as Pru and try to explain it away? *Not to this town.*

Quite a few folk didn't much care for Pru's no-nonsense attitude and sometimes her outspokenness offended people, but she was generous, very generous — like her father before her — and no one had any complaints about that.

Besides, Judge Ivers and most of the town councillors would feel it was their bounden duty to run her killer to ground and exact full vengeance.

There would be no easy way of explaining how she died, and another gunshot now, so long after the last one would make it virtually impossible to get away with it. He would need a much better story than the spur-of-the-moment lies he had told Pru: he had seen she was suspicious almost right away. And then the damn kid had rallied long enough to tell her what had really happened!

Goddamnit! It had blown-up in his face!

There was no way out: he simply couldn't let her live. But if he killed her now, how *could* he possibly explain it?

It would be damned hard and he would be under suspicion whatever story he told. Which meant he would have to run, and any posse that came after him would be sure to be led by Cody.

That son of a bitch had been a thorn in his side ever since arriving in Hopeful! He would be relentless in hunting down Ross . . . relentless!

The only way to stop him would be to kill him and that would mean setting up an ambush along the trail. But the rest of the posse would still be there to continue the pursuit, afterward.

Whatever happened, it was all over for him here in Hopeful. '*Hopeless*' would be a better name!

All his plans were gone now, thanks to Cody.

Then, as Pru gathered her senses and started to get up, he instinctvely took her arm and helped her to her feet. She swayed in against him — and suddenly a cold smile split his worried face. He knew *just* what to do now!

12

Bait

Cody was groggy when they awakened him in the hotel room. He was still weak from his fever, but Doc Timmins had insisted on him taking some laudanum last night before turning in so as to ease any pain during the night.

Now Cody felt only half-sensible, weak, sluggish and hazy in thought and movement, as a result of the sedative pain-killer.

He blinked, groped for the cup of coffee Judge Ivers handed him. There were three armed men behind the judge and Cody squinted, recognizing two of them as hands from Block R who had come to town to help control any lynch mob. He shook his head a little, sipped the hot coffee.

'What goes on, Judge?'

'There have been quite a few developments overnight, Cody. No need to worry about a lynch mob any longer: Red Higgins was found shot dead in his cell, and young Chip Garner is very badly wounded, may not see out the day.'

Cody's brain started to kick in and he straightened, forced himself to stand and drink more coffee.

The judge steadied him. 'Chip managed to tell Doc that Red was killed by Ross, who also shot Chip. Pru turned up while Ross was rigging things to make it look as if Chip had been careless and allowed Ross to get hold of a gun.'

'Yeah, I can see how Ross would try to turn things around — but why? What made him go off the rails?'

'It appears that he and Red Higgins had some past dealings and Ross arranged the bank robbery while all the town was at Nate Palmer's funeral. Red was going to spill everything to save his own neck. Chip heard it all.'

Cody had to sit down again, asked one of the cowboys to roll him a cigarette: his own hands were still fumbling.

'Pru?'

'That's the crux of the matter, Cody. Ross has gone on the run, and taken Pru along as hostage.'

Cody said nothing, sat there on the edge of the bed, staring at the floor. He took the cigarette the cowhand had rolled for him, nodded his thanks, and bent his head towards the match the man held ready. Exhaling, he looked up through the smoke.

'I think Ross'll use Pru as bait — he figures he's got a lot to square with me. How much start does he have?'

'We're not sure. A Mexican girl from the diner taking breakfast to the jail discovered Chip, barely alive — this was just after sun up and Chip, hardly able to speak, didn't know just when Ross had left. But there'd been a shouting match between a couple of drunks — two of those men Pru fired earlier

— and some hotel guests. The clerk said Pru went out, just after — round about midnight, he thinks.'

'You'll have to help me out, Judge. Brain's not firin' too well. Where's this going?'

Ivers tightened his mouth a little with impatience, but realized Cody was still recovering from the laudanum's sedative effect.

'Well, it would appear Pru had been awakened by the shouting between the drunks and the guests and *probably*, then decided to go down to the jail. She'd be worried about young Chip. You know how she likes to fuss over him.'

Cody nodded. 'So I've heard. I get it now — sorry I'm so slow, but starting to come good. You got a posse organized?'

'I have some men gathering volunteers. D'you feel up to leading it?'

'Sure.'

Judge Ivers smiled thinly. 'You could have fooled me, but maybe you're just pretending to look as if you've been riding all night, trying to stop a stampede.'

'I've had worse hangovers, Judge. I'll wash up and by the time I'm dressed, I'll be ready to ride.' He glanced towards the man who had given him the cigarette. 'Can you get my hoss saddled for me, Cres?'

'Sure, Cody. Judge, we'll get the men together at the livery and wait for you and Cody to show up. That OK?'

Ivers agreed and the armed men left. 'Look, Cody, you're the best man to lead, I know, but there's no sense in pushing yourself too hard in this. I can already see a little blood showing through your head bandage.'

'From tossing and turning on the pillow. Doc warned me it might happen. Nothin' to worry about. Show me the wash-up bench, Judge, we're losing time.'

The posse left town forty minutes later and Cody was looking much better. He claimed he felt fine, his usual self, but more than one man noted the way he gripped his chestnut with his knees and had the reins wrapped around his left wrist so as to give him more stability in the saddle.

There were ten men — ten *grim* men — in the posse. Judge Ivers had chosen them from families who had benefited in some way from Pru's past generosity and hoped they would persevere and keep on until Blake Ross was run down and captured, or killed, and hopefully, Pru would be returned alive and well.

There had been some delay while Cody, considerably freshened after his wash, had rousted the town gunmaker and asked if he could borrow a Sharps Big Fifty rifle. 'With a flip-up Vernier-scale sight on the rear.'

'Man, I've got three rifles in stock, only one fitted with a Vernier. New Sharps are scarce now: there ain't so many buffalo around and price of hides has gone down, and the calibre's too big for regular game,' the man complained, whining. 'Too expensive for the ordinary man.' He was lean as a wire, expert at his trade, according to Ivers, but tight with a dollar. 'Feller was in last week from Wyoming, says there's a big migration of buff across the Laramie Plains. Hunters are movin' in from all over, like it might be the last chance for years to make a fast buck. They'll all be lookin' for guns. If someone down here wants to go try for his fortune and I don't have a Sharps to sell him, I'll be the poorer.'

'Three Sharps won't make you rich, Mr Retallick.'

The raw-boned man hesitated, then nodded. 'Possibly not — and Pru has given me good custom over the years, I suppose. Very well, Mr Cody. We'll make a deal: I've some hand-loaded ammunition I can offer.' He gave a quick, on-off smile. 'Just a sweetener for someone who may be indecisive.'

To Cody, it sounded as if the man had set a premium on his three buffalo rifles because of their scarcity — it was even possible that the talk of a mass migration of buffalo across the Laramie Plains was merely a contrivance to bring in buyers and clear stock that had been gathering dust on Retallick's shelves.

Cody kept his thoughts to himself. But when the gunmaker asked for a ten-dollar deposit on the rifle, plus the cost of a box of ten hand-loaded shells, he figured he was right about Retallick's concern with profit. He scooped up the box of big cartridges and the rifle before the man could protest. 'Put it on the town council's account.'

'I-I don't run accounts, sir! This is strictly a cash-on-the-barrelhead business, so I must ask you to — '

But Retallick was speaking to a closed door with Cody on the other side walking back to where the posse waited.

Judge Ivers smiled when he saw the big rifle. He glanced back at the gunshop where Retallick was now standing holding the door, looking hang-dog anxious.

'I do believe you've accomplished something that no one else in this town has managed.' At Cody's querying look, the judge added, 'You've talked Isaiah Retallick into lending you that rifle without leaving a deposit.'

'Well, wouldn't say I'd talked him into it, just moved a mite faster, that's all.'

The posse men who heard chuckled.

'He'll be wringin' his fingers clear off his hands!' someone ventured.

★   ★   ★

Cody checked with the livery man for what kind of horse Ross was riding.

'Aw, guess he's forkin' his usual mount, a calico stallion with a wild eye. Been at him for a long while to change it for a geldin' or a mare. Sooner or later he's gonna be ridin' along nice and peaceful and that calico's gonna get a whiff of a mare in season on the wind, and he'll take off like an arrer from an Injun's huntin' bow.'

'Yeah, that can happen — but what about tracks? Any unusual things, like throwing out the left forefoot, nicked hind shoe, or some such . . . ?'

The livery man shook his head. 'Nah, nothin' that easy — but one thing: Blake rides close-up on the withers. Likes to sit forward in his saddle. Like a bareback Injun does, you know?'

Cody nodded: the forehoofs would leave a slightly deeper mark than the rear: it was something to watch for.

'Know what mount he put the woman on?'

Again the stable man shook his head. 'They keep a coupla spares in the stables behind the law office — a grey and a claybank, if memory serves. Just stand-in mounts, nothin' special about 'em. Claybank's the faster, I reckon, which ain't sayin' a whole helluva lot.'

Cody thanked the man and joined the waiting posse.

Cres Ballard from Block R said Ross would probably take the north-west trail once he cleared town.

'It leads to the hills and the badlands,' the cowboy explained. 'Roughly in the direction of that area where Chip found you. Best place to hide if you're on the run, or gonna try an' jump a freight.'

'Everyone know that?'

'Hell, yeah, first place anyone makes for if he's on the dodge . . . ' Cres's words slowly trailed off as he saw Cody's face. 'Oh-oh! So Ross'd mebbe choose another trail.'

'He could still turn it around. Let us figure he'd go someplace else, but *still* make for those hills and leave us with egg on our faces. He's moving fast now, knows he'll be hounded to hell and back because of Pru. He left Chip for dead without checkin' to make sure, but he won't take any more chances. So, what're our choices, Cres?'

Ballard wasn't afraid to admit he needed help in such a decision and conferred with the others, all local men, five, including Cres, from the surrounding ranches, the rest from town or close-in farms.

They all came up with suggestions

and Cody noticed that the river trail seemed to have more supporters than other directions.

'Where will that take him?' Cody asked.

Ballard spoke slowly, considering his answer. 'If Ross heads out through the forest, he's goin' away from the railroad. It's a good distance from here whichever way you go, but it's furthest by way of the woods. If he's a notion to try and jump a freight — which would be his best bet — the river trail'd be better.'

Some men agreed, two others flatly refused to consider anything but the forest, yet another changed his mind and agreed with Cres.

'Now where the hell does that leave us?' growled one of the men who figured the forest was the best way for Ross to take. 'He goes by the river and he's only got the crossin' at Badger's Ferry to take him into wild country, which he has to cross if he wants to come up with the railroad. He goes by way of the cattle trails and he'll run into too much company. You ask me he *has* to go through the forest.'

'River ferry sounds possible,' Cody allowed. 'If he crosses, where does it take him?'

He looked to Cres again for an answer and the cowboy hesitated, frowning. 'He'd likely head for the Signal Breaks as the shortest way through, but that's Indian country and they still ain't *hospitable* to us palefaces.'

A man Cody knew only as Skillet, a farmer from the basin outside of Hopeful, spoke up. 'I been sodbustin' a long time now, but before I took up my land in the basin, I worked as a logger up in the Breaks. Recollect the straw boss tellin' us not to worry none about any Injuns we seen, 'cause they wouldn't bother us — '

Someone scoffed. 'Was you awake when he told you that hogwash?'

'Bright-eyed and ready to howl,' Skillet answered, amiably, spitting a brown stream of tobacco juice. ''Cause why? 'Cause we was loggin' for *Brock Riordan*, Pru's old man, and he was always partial to Injuns, seen 'em right, sent in beeves and corn when they was starvin'.' He lowered his voice and added, 'Was said he had a little squaw up there, too.'

'Wouldn't mind visitin' a couple of them young Kiowa squaws, meself,' another farmer said, 'but what you gettin' at, Skillet?'

Skillet looked exasperated. 'Who the hell you think Ross is ridin' with, you dumb sodbuster? No wonder we got a rep for bein' thick between the ears among cowmen. He's got *Pru Riordan* with him! Old Brock's daughter!'

That caused some discussion: would Blake Ross ride through there with Pru, make up some wild story about men who wanted to harm her on her trail, so the Indians would help them because she was Old Man Riordan's daughter? He would have to make sure Pru never got a chance to speak, or even looked like a prisoner. Or, as a last resort he might even use her to *make* the Indians help, or he would harm her.

All mighty risky, desperation moves, but Ross was desperate. So, either way, the posse could be in trouble.

'Before we waste time arguing that out,' Cody said, turning again to Cres Ballard, 'would Ross know about the Injuns favouring Riordan?'

'Might,' Cres said slowly. 'I've heard of it. It's bandied about as gossip sometimes, by old-timers around the cracker-barrel kind of thing. Most folk believe it's true, others say Old Brock'd never've took a squaw.'

'Forget that part,' Cody said. 'Did he give them beef and corn when they were starving?'

It was agreed Old Man Riordan had indeed made this friendly gesture and Cody stood immediately. 'Saddle up — it's worth a try. In any case, we'll pick up word at the ferry if Ross crossed the river.'

Just to be on the safe side, he sent two men — cowhands with the fastest horses in the posse — to check out the north-west trail through the forest, in case Ross had pulled a smart one.

The rest headed along the river and reached the ferry before sundown. Cody had searched for tracks along the way and figured in two or three places there were hoofmarks that could have been made by Ross's calico, but the ground was too crumbly to be certain.

In any case, the ferryman confirmed that Ross and Pru Riordan had crossed the river on his barge just before noon, taken two of his horses he hired out to passengers at gunpoint.

'Likely gonna trade 'em to the Injuns,' the man said bitterly.

'Still got a damn good start,' Cody said, a mite worried about that fact. 'The woman seem OK?'

The ferryman snorted. 'Hands raw-hided to the saddlehorn, no hat — I'd say she was less than *OK!*'

The Breaks looked mighty rugged and brooding as the sun slanted westward, leaving them full of moving dark shadows.

'Skillet, you reckon you can still find your way around in here?'

'Come daylight I might be able to locate the old loggin' camp — been deserted for years.'

'Not waiting till daylight. We'll have some grub, rest up a spell, and be riding again before midnight. Moon's still big enough to give us light to see by.'

'Yeah! Be light enough for someone lyin' in ambush to pick us off, too!' a townsman observed. He was named Little, but it didn't suit him. He was pickaxe-handle broad across the shoulders, mid-thirties, and had corded muscles on his thick forearms, displayed because his shirt sleeves were rolled-up. He worked in the storehouse at the stage depot, and had been mostly surly on the ride so far.

'Ross'd be a fool to try an ambush,' Cody told him shortly. 'We'll spread out. Skillet can tell us the most likely way Ross would go to get through the Breaks. We'll converge on some landmark, have a pow-wow. You know of a good place, Skillet?'

'Mmm. Mebbe a rock arch: ride under an' you're on the way outa the hills. Base of a basalt spire — you can see it a couple miles away.'

'Everyone happy with that?'

'Hell, no! I din' 'spect this kind of thing!' Little complained. 'Full daylight work I was ready for, but this prowlin' through the Breaks, of all godforsaken places, in the dark ain't for me.' He paused, shook his head. 'Pru Riordan never done all that much for me!'

'Go back, then,' Cody told him curtly, reaching for another piece of cold venison from the pile on the platter.

'What?'

'I said, go back. You're no use to me with that attitude, friend.' Cody raked his gaze around the others. 'Anyone else feels the same can join him. I need men committed to this chore, committed to saving Pru Riordan, not conditional on how much grub she put on your table, or which clothes she bought for your kids. That's a miserable way to look at things.'

Little stood abruptly, trail-reddened eyes angry, big fists bunched down at his sides. 'That's the same as callin' a man yaller!'

'Well, a man thinks that way, ain't much better'n yaller,' Cody said calmly, watching Little's face redden. 'I'm not appealing to your consciences: you already know what's the right thing to do — or should. Just make your decisions by the time supper's finished.'

'You gonna let us split up?' someone asked uncertainly.

'Rather have a few committed men than an army that's bitchin' all the time and ain't got its mind of the chore.'

When Little growled and made his move, Cody was ready. He rose swiftly, dodged the first wild blow — which might well have taken his head off his shoulders had it connected! — and crouched under the big swinging arm. He came up inside that arm and Little jumped back, startled — just at the right range for Cody to whip up his Colt and slam it hard alongside the man's head.

Little just stood there, grunted, blinked, then reached for Cody's neck. But Cody stepped back this time and the man's legs folded and Little spread out on the ground. Cody holstered the gun, sat down and dusted off his slice of venison, chewing.

'I'll go this alone if I have to,' he told them.

They knew it was no idle boast, but there were still some men who reneged on their first commitment. Cody savvied how they felt — family men, all: what would happen to their wives and kids if they didn't return?

Pru Riordan didn't hold that big a slice of their loyalty or gratitude, it seemed, but that was for them to wrestle with on sleepless nights.

There were only four men left, including Cody, when it came time to move. Cody, Cres Ballard, Skillet and the big man with a sore head who belied his name — Vern Little.

The others rode out silently, not looking at the men who were continuing the pursuit of Blake Ross and Pru.

'How's the head?' Cody asked Little, as Skillet pointed the way into the Breaks.

'Damn sore. I'll square with you on that.'

'Leave it 'til after we get Pru Riordan back.'

Little smiled crookedly. 'Guess I can do that. You're a son of a bitch, you know, the way you prod a man's conscience.'

'As long as it works, you can call me worse than a sonofabitch and I won't even miss a drag on my cigarette.'

'I'm workin' on it already.'

'Fine. But now, let's find out where Ross is headed.'

13

Long Shot

The small posse rendezvoused at the rock arch as arranged, but there was only Vern Little with Cody now. Skillet and Cres Ballard had gone off scouting — Cres said he recalled a small cabin on the slope above the sawpits where Ross could hole-up with his hostage.

'Ross'll know about it, 'cause he and Nat Palmer once trapped a couple wideloopers there,' Cres told Cody.

'You see sign of 'em, you come fetch me,' Cody said, not liking to split the group any more. 'I don't want to shoot that cabin full of holes, then go in and find Pru dead right alongside Ross.'

'One of us'll stay to watch the cabin if there's any sign of life, Cody,' Cres assured him. 'T'other'll come fetch you.'

So they split again, and Vern Little climbed up on an old rotting loading platform, staying in the shadow cast by a still-standing tree, and slowly ran his gaze over the ruins of the logging camp.

Cody made his own surveillance, tensely, wondering if they had done right to stop here and not pass right on through to the trail that would eventually lead to the railroad.

But, as on countless hunts in the mountains, he had learned that steady stalking paid off in the long run. He stiffened at a hissing sound from Little, saw the man crouching low by the lone tree.

'Cody! There's a ledge above the mill ruins — hard to see but I know it's there. It's a fine lookout point. I think someone's up there.'

Cody was beside him in a moment, down on one knee, hand tightening around the rifle. Little pointed and he strained to see but couldn't make out the ledge. He was about to snap at the other in frustration when suddenly the shadows resolved themselves — and he saw the darker, jutting line across the paleness of the grey rock cliff.

'See the ledge but no movement.'

'Somethin' there — kind of a flash. No, not even that — like dim light hitting metal, somethin' small.'

'Like a gun?' Cody's mouth was dry as he asked.

'Smaller. Mebbe a belt buckle . . . hey I heard somethin' then!'

'So did I! Dull thud — something dropping.'

'Would Ross be that clumsy?'

Before Cody could answer, there came a woman's piercing scream, slashing through the dull moonlight, sending a brace of nightbirds flapping chaotically from a cliffside nest.

* * *

Ross knew now it had been a mistake bringing Pru along, but at the time couldn't think of anything else to do.

A woman-killer stood no chance on

the frontier — women of all kinds were too scarce. But he made good time to the Breaks. He and Nate Palmer had hunted wideloopers here a year ago. *He'd give any posse a damn run for their money!*

But Pru was a hellcat: he should've expected it, the way she strutted about like she was queen of the range. He had felt her slim, firm body through her clothing as he had lifted her down, let his hands linger and wander. Still bound, she had kicked him where it *hurt*.

Now, he stood on the high ledge and levered a shell into the rifle breech as he waited for the girl to get up off the ground where she had fallen after he had struck her.

Pru, dazed, her head ringing and the left side of her face feeling as if she had been slapped by a pine plank, struggled awkwardly to a sitting position, her hands still bound in front of her. She tasted blood and fought to bring her vision into focus.

Ross waited, standing mostly in shadow. She couldn't see his face but his contempt for her was clear in his voice.

'Been wantin' to do that for a long time. Bet if you get right down to it, half the town'd like to take a swing at you.'

Pru said nothing: lately she had come to realize she was far too outspoken, but that came of growing up without a mother's guiding hand. Her father had been a terse, demanding man, hiding any affection he had beneath his clipped speech.

She had inherited his impatience, wanted things done pronto, and this reflected in her voice and manner. She had also inherited her father's generous streak, although he had always made a pretence of being reluctant, but was secretly pleased to do something for folks less fortunate, or even the town in general, like building a schoolhouse and a church.

She knew full well that the townsfolk

only tolerated her bossy manner because of these things. At times she had been on the very edge of apologizing for her manner, but always told herself she didn't *need* their approval. But, lately, she had been more amiable and admitted to herself that she preferred this. She didn't realize it, but Pru was maturing, and beginning to savvy she didn't need to boss people around so much. Maybe Catamount Cody had had something to do with that.

But right now, she was in the hands of Blake Ross and he had a valid reason for his antagonistic attitude: apart from that recent kick, she had been very vocal about not posting him as sheriff of Hopeful.

'You got my message yet? You do what I say, when I say it and you don't gimme no backchat, or next time you'll be missing some teeth.'

Feeling the rock pressing into her back, she nodded, hair spilling across her face. Her heart was hammering: she had never been struck by a man before and it wasn't an experience she wanted to repeat. She was afraid: fear wasn't a usual emotion with Pru, though there had been a few times in her life when she had felt wrenching terror — when drunken, break-out Indians had cornered her and two of her men in a box canyon and set fire to the brush, their companions blocking the only exit; the river crossing with a trail herd, a placid shallow ford, that had become a raging death-trap with a flash flood, thousands of gallons of water washing away cows and men and wagons. They had found her a mile downstream, five feet up in the branches of a tree when the flood had finally subsided.

Those had been times of real fear and this moment, she had to admit, was yet another.

'You kill me and they'll hunt you down . . . Blake,' she gasped.

He surprised her by laughing, short and harsh, never taking his eyes off the distant shadowed and moon-splotched landscape.

'What you think they're doin' now? Gonna catch up with me and shake my hand? I'm a dead man if Cody gets within rifle shot, I know that, but it won't matter to you. When he shows, you're dead.'

'Is — Isn't that rather foolish? You could use me to . . . to barter your way out of a tight spot.'

He turned to glare at her, mouth twisting slowly. 'I got you really scared, ain't I? By hell, that gives me a good feelin'. Like in a cathouse, when I slap around one of the chippies and she starts beggin' for me to stop. *Yeah!* It feels just like that!'

He seemed surprised, but Pru's fear increased and she pressed back harder against the wall. She felt her bladder was ready to burst when he took a step towards her and stood looking down, towering above her. She could not hold back the small whimper when one rough hand lifted strands of her hair and fondled it. *Oh, God! First the hair, then what?*

227

Suddenly he squatted in front of her and she felt her eyes widen as his fingers fumbled the top button of her blouse. She tried to back away — *impossible!* — as his hand slid under the cloth, his fingers groping.

His breath was hissing through his nostrils. 'Man! I wonder if I got time . . . ?'

He spoke aloud, but she knew the words weren't meant for her. He was trying to convince himself that he could assault her before Cody showed up. *Oh, dear God! She was only surmising Cody would come! But there was no real proof yet that there was a posse on their trail . . .*

There would be one, she was sure, but not necessarily in this area of the bleak and doom-laden Signal Breaks. She had always hated this place, had avoided it as much as she could and was glad when the logging camp closed so she didn't have to ride up here with her father.

Now, here she was, a prisoner of a

killer, on the ledge above the ruins of that very logging camp.

Ross stepped back now and she could hear his breathing — it was *heavier* — and he tapped horny fingernails against his big teeth, studying her. Then he turned and slowly scanned the country below as far as he could see.

She felt sick when he leaned the rifle against the rock and took off his six-gun rig, let it drop at his feet.

He grinned tightly at her as he fumbled with the big brass buckle of his trouser belt.

Go on! she told herself, *You've got nothing to lose!* So, she screamed. Piercingly. Echoing, splintering the night . . .

* * *

Vern Little took one hell of a chance — why he did it, Cody would never savvy. To give Cody the time he needed to get up to the ledge, even as the echoes of Pru's scream bounced from wall to wall, Little ran to his mount and leapt into the saddle.

Vern's spurs raked, he slid his Winchester from the saddle scabbard and he cut loose with a rebel yell that drowned Pru's scream entirely.

The rifle came up to his shoulder, long legs almost straight down in the lengthened stirrups so that he was virtually standing while still riding. He aimed high, shooting fast, but knew there was little chance of hitting any particular target. But for now, the main thing was *distraction*.

Sparks erupted in swiftly blossoming orange flowers, walking in a ragged line across the cliff face above the ledge. Over the thunder of his mount's hoofs he heard the buzz and whine and snarl of the lead spinning away into the night. He caught a brief sound and his heart skipped a beat — it sounded like Pru had screamed again. *Hell! If one of the ricochets had hit her*. He guided the horse around the rocky base, then clamped teeth down on the reins while he emptied the rest of his magazine against the rock face now towering above him.

But the racing horse stepped wrong on that broken ground and he heard another *crack!* close by — the mount's left foreleg snapping. The animal whinnied shrilly and was going down in a nose dive even as Vern tried to kick his boots free of the stirrups. But his full weight was on them and the ground rose to meet him. He was flung almost eight feet — a normal sized man would have made ten or more — and then he hit and the world exploded in a series of bright explosions, the light sucked swiftly into impenetrable blackness. He didn't hear the mount's neck snap, or feel the crushing weight as the horse rolled on top of him.

Vern Little's ride had started — and ended — so abruptly that Cody had scant time to make a plan. It was the right response: Vern's instant reaction to the scream was exactly what Ross

231

would expect. He must know Cody was out there somewhere, no matter how much he tried to tell himself that the man wouldn't come into the Breaks until daylight. But Ross had not counted on Vern, a man who had worked and knew this rugged country. The wild ride and the raking shots were the reactions of a desperate man, and Ross must have been grinning to himself when he heard the horse go down, the unmistakable sliding and roiling dust of a mighty serious fall. *So much for Cody!*

By that time, though, Cody was climbing the cliff face.

The weight of the Sharps buffalo gun was dragging at him, although he slipped the rawhide sling over his shoulder. The heavy cartridges in his jacket pocket tended to pull him down on one side as he released his grip with one hand and lunged for another. Once again he found a new solid grip, fingertips aching as they strained. His boots located footholds that supported his weight.

But it was an eerie feeling, moving upwards, his face inches from the basalt and yet unable to see it. All he could make out was a dark-grey blur and only when his cheek scraped the rough surface did he feel the upward motion and knew he wasn't floundering in some kind of weird dream.

The echoes of Little's shooting were dying away now, and small stones and grit trickled down. They hit the stiff brim of Cody's hat and — *rattled*. He stopped, hanging in dark space, literally, by his fingertips.

Then, from above, came words that chilled him.

'Well, I'll be! *Hey!* Who dat down dere?' A chuckle. 'Wouldn't be you, Cody, old man, would it?'

Ross must've seen him clinging to the cliff face, looking straight down, dark against the lighter ground, now twelve feet below him.

Cody tried to deaden the sound of his heavy breathing by plunging his face into the sweat-wet sleeve of his jacket.

Again the stiff felt brim of his hat let him down: it bent against the rock face, tilted on to the back of his head, and fell into the darkness.

'My, my! I guess the Good Lord is favourin' me tonight! Aw, Cody, it's a dead shame you can't see what a fine target your head makes with that bandage showin' all white an' sittin' there like a nestin' dove!'

A gun roared and a bullet zipped past Cody's face so close he smelled the hot powder grains clinging to the lead.

Up on the ledge Ross swore, but not too hotly: he knew he had plenty of time and there was nothing Cody could do to hide the paleness of that bandage. He took his time, aiming. Then Pru's riding boots drove against his spine and hurtled him out into space. He yelled as he fell and one of his flailing arms struck Cody's shoulder and tore loose his arm. Cody kicked away from the wall and he and Ross hit the slope, twelve feet below, at almost the same time.

Cody ducked out from under the Sharps' sling and let the heavy gun fall. His legs felt as if they were driving up under his jaw. Breath blasted from him and he dived forward towards the dim flailing shape a couple yards away.

Ross was staggering up when Cody drove his head into the man's midriff, wrapped his arms about his hips and they went down in a tangle of limbs and thudding fists.

Cody was first to his knees, hammered a blow into Ross's mouth. The thick lips split against the man's teeth and he spat in Cody's face. Then he scooped up a handful of dirt, flung it after the spittle, groped again for a rock or stone big enough to beat Cody's head in. He cursed the impulse that had made him drop his six-gun and cartridge belt on the ledge and then Cody came out of the darkness, hooking him on the side of the neck, driving an elbow against his ear.

Roaring with the pain, Ross reared up, lifted a knee that took Cody in the chest, hammered several blows down on to the man's back, ripped off the betraying bandage and clawed his fingers into the head wound. Cody shouted in pain as the edges were torn open and blood flowed. Blindly, he forked his fingers and struck out.

Ross screamed as horny nails probed into his left eye. He twisted away, staggering, hands to his face. Somehow he kept his feet, although he was like a drunk in a Texas twister. Then he felt the ground levelling — and heard the close-by whinny of a horse.

Groping hands found saddle and stirrups and the warm hide of a mount. It backed away but he clung to the horn, dancing on one leg, the other boot groping for the stirrup. He yelled triumphantly as he swung up into saddle, slapped the reins free from the anchoring stone and spurred away . . .

Cody, half-blinded by blood from his head wound, groped his way up to the ledge, guided by Pru's voice. He had her hands free in a moment and she tore off his neckerchief, bound it over his head, using her own, smaller neckerchief to wipe the blood from his eyes.

'You all right?' Cody gasped.

'I am . . . now. But it was very close.' She shuddered and put a hand on his arm. 'Thank you. I-I don't know what else to say.'

'That says it all.' They were at the base of the cliff now and he picked up the big Sharps, blowing dirt from the action. Then he began looking around, straining to see. She thought he was searching for signs of Blake Ross.

'Ross is getting away . . . '

'We'll catch him, don't worry. Can you see Vern?'

It took only a couple of minutes to find the dead horse with Little pinned underneath by one leg. Cody thought he was dead but Little gasped, 'Get this jughead offa me!'

They dug away the soft earth and pulled Little free. One leg was broken and Pru set about splinting it with lengths of short saplings.

'You hadn't addled my brain with that gun-whippin', I'd've had the son of a bitch!'

'You would've, too. I promise I'll never gunwhip you again.'

Even though in pain, Vern chuckled.

Cres and Skillet found their way to them and they decided to simply camp where they were for the night and look for Ross in daylight.

'From what he said, I think he's trying to get aboard the early freight train, bound for Federation,' Pru told them. 'He's unarmed, anyway. He left his six-gun on the ledge and must've lost his rifle in the fall.'

Cody shook his head. 'My Winchester was in the saddle scabbard on my horse.'

The men came alert at once, looking around them swiftly. 'We better mount guards,' Cres said, and offered to take first duty.

They were all grateful for the chance to sleep.

It semed like only minutes later when

Cody was roughly shaken awake. Skillet was bending over him. It was almost sun-up, already light enough to see the grime in the coarse pores of Skillet's face.

'I just seen a rider — has to be Ross.' He pointed off to the left, through the rock arch and down the narrow valley, the way out of the Breaks to the distant railroad.

Stiff, seeing Pru and the others stirring at the rumbling sound of Skillet's voice, Cody clambered to his feet. Skillet handed him the big Sharps.

'Cody, be careful,' Pru cautioned.

He smiled and climbed into the saddle of Cres's bay. He held the Sharps across his knees as he rode away, Skillet reaching for the reins of his own mount, calling, 'You won't reach him in time, Cody! Lookit! There's the smoke of the freight above yonder hill. He'll beat you by a mile!'

'This gun'll shoot a mile!' Cody said, spurring away.

Ross, too, had seen the smoke from

the freight's bell-shaped stack and was flailing at the chestnut with the rein ends, driving it full tilt towards the railroad tracks, now glowing like burning streaks of gold in the rising sun.

The dark blob of the locomotive appeared, rocking and swaying as it rounded the bend. Cody heard the distant drifting wail of the whistle, a puff of steam whipping away.

Ross was closing fast, making for a small rise that would slow the train enough for him to transfer on board. He was the best part of a mile distant.

Cody looked around as the bay raced out of the Breaks and he wheeled abruptly, running it for a nest of boulders halfway up a rise. The horse whinnied when Cody skidded it to a stop and hit the ground running. He clambered up to a big rock he had noticed that was reasonably flat on top. Panting, sweating, he tore off his corduroy jacket, rolled it swiftly and then stretched out, laying the fore end of the Sharps across the bundle.

The ungiving rock was uncomfortable, but he flipped up the Vernier scale peep-sight, watched Ross ramming the chestnut in a desperate bid to reach the train while it was still labouring up the grade.

About twelve . . . twelve-and-a-half hundred yards. He was using a strange gun and wouldn't even have time for a ranging shot.

He set the scale, snugged the brass-bound butt firmly into his shoulder. He already had a long cartridge in the breech, cocked the big side-hammer and took his sighting. His eye watered with the strain as he sought Ross. He snatched a breath, held it, and saw the killer standing in the stirrups, ready to launch himself at an open-bed freight car stacked with cut-and-dressed timber. He led him by two feet.

The man must be feeling mighty pleased now that success was well within his grasp. The big gun boomed, its thunder rolling and cracking across the countryside. Cody's body was pushed back violently a good ten inches and he dropped the gun, grabbing at his throbbing shoulder. He struggled to his knees, then to his feet, shading his eyes.

Ross was standing on the chestnut's saddle, giving himself more height, legs slightly bent. He leapt and Cody swore bitterly. *Too damn late.*

But Ross hadn't *leapt*: he had been propelled by the .56 calibre bullet, hurling him violently against the side of the freight wagon. The train lost absolutely no speed at all as Ross fell and its wheels rolled over his limp body.

★   ★   ★

'Man who can shoot that good just has to make a fine sheriff,' Vern Little wheezed, back in the camp they had made by a shaded stream on the edge of the Signal Breaks. His leg was splinted and he was sitting up, drinking coffee brewed by Pru. 'Don't you reckon, fellers?'

Skillet grunted and Cres said, 'How

about it, Cody?'

He glanced at Pru, who watched soberly, but with something new in her eyes — maybe urging him to say yes?

'I'll give it some thought. Once I get the bounty money away to Chicago for Lurlene, I'll be needing a job then.'

'Hope you'll pick up the sheriff's badge, Cody,' Cres said. 'We'd all like that, wouldn't we, Pru?'

She didn't care for one of her cowhands putting her on the spot like that, but smiled slowly and, speaking straight to Cody, said, 'I'm . . . 'hopeful'.'

'That seems fitting.' He grinned, sipped some more strong coffee.

THE END

Other titles in the
Linford Western Library:

DALTON'S MISSION

Ed Law

Dalton and Loren Steele happen across an ambushed gold shipment where everyone dies, attackers and defenders alike. They try to return the gold to Perry Haynes of the Durando Mining Company, its rightful owner, but Perry has been overthrown. Gun law and corruption reign in Durando and both men are jailed — charged with stealing the very gold they've rescued! Now, to reclaim Perry's mine, Dalton and Steele must strap on their six-shooters and tame the hell-hole that is Durando.

ARIZONA PAY-OFF

Duke Patterson

When Tex Scarron, six feet of whipcord and steel, rides home to the Bar X in Arizona, he finds Parson Dean and his gang working a lucrative 'protection' racket. Ranchers who fail to pay up find that their cattle are rustled, their homesteads are burnt down and their cowhands are shot in the back. As Tex sets out to rid the territory of the Parson, his experience of fighting hoodlums comes in handy when the gunplay gets fast and furious.

GUN LAW

Lee Walker

Aged fourteen, Jake Chalmers witnessed his parents' murder by drunken cowboys. Now he's a young man — with a gun for protection . . . On the run after killing, in self-defence, Jake arrives in Sweetwater. But he's unable to maintain a low profile when he becomes embroiled in a feud between the businessman Jordan Carter, and sheriff Luke Gardner. Then one of Carter's men murders Luke, and Jake must choose between the law of the land and the law of the gun . . .

SIX FOR LARAMIE

Rick Dalmas

Six gun-fighters come to Laramie — all hungry for money. Yet greed is not everyone's sole motive. Bannerman, the toughest and fastest, has a special reason: one of the other five has shot his friend in the back. There's no charge for what he intends to do to him, even though he knows this might disrupt the plans for the work he's been hired to do — and that it could put him on the wrong end of *five* guns!

GUN FURY

Walt Keene

When veteran gunfighter Tom Dix and his pal Dan Shaw get a telegraph message from the remote town of Gun Fury, it's from their friend Wild Bill Hickok. Realising that something perilous is brewing they saddle up and ride. Death awaits them when they reach Gun Fury — bodies soon start to pile up. Curiously, the infamous Hickok claims he never sent for them. But Dix and Shaw are trapped in Gun Fury — and fighting for their lives . . .

COWTOWN KIDNAP

James Martell

When Slim Petersen overhears kidnap plans, involving the son of one of the Vargo boys, he fails to convince the brothers of the plot — until there's an attempt upon his own life. Then, despite him working to thwart the kidnappers, it seems that the outlaws' plans are working. One Vargo dies and another is taken prisoner. Slim has help when he faces the renegades in a final, explosive showdown. Men die and he frees the prisoner — but can he survive?